Time for a Change

The four of us spent the night in a foul-smelling concrete-block cell. Then the next morning we got hauled before a justice of the peace who let the men, including Pa, off for time served and a promise they'd leave town promptly.

We were going out the door when he called me back. "You! The young one."

"Yes, sir?"

"Wait a minute," he said, as he hunted through a newspaper. He tore out a piece and motioned for me to take it. "Can you read?"

"Sure."

"Don't tell me 'sure.' Lots can't. Anyway, read that before you hop another freight train. It's about the CCC's fall enrollment. It's not too late to sign up."

Pa had followed me back in, and now he said, "CCC! Moss is too good for welfare and he knows it. Moss, you come with me."

"Take a hard look at your father," the JP said. "Is that how you want to turn out? Like him?"

Pa stalked off, and after a moment, I followed.

No, I didn't want to turn out like him. Not like he was now, anyway.

Hitch

Other Books by Jeanette Ingold

Hitch

Jeanette Ingold

HARCOURT, INC.
Orlando   Austin   New York
San Diego   Toronto   London

For information about permission to reproduce selections from this book,
write to trade.permissions@hmhco.com or to Permissions,
Houghton Mifflin Harcourt Publishing Company,
3 Park Avenue, 19th Floor, New York, New York 10016.

www.hmhco.com

First Harcourt paperback edition 2006

The Library of Congress has cataloged the hardcover edition as follows:
Ingold, Jeanette.
Hitch/Jeanette Ingold.
p. cm.
Summary: To help his family during the Depression and avoid
becoming a drunk like his father, Moss Trawnley joins the Civilian
Conservation Corps, helps build a new camp near Monroe, Montana,
and leads the other men in making the camp a success.
1. Civilian Conservation Corps (U.S.)—Juvenile fiction.
[1. Civilian Conservation Corps (U.S.)—Fiction.
2. Conservation of natural resources—Fiction.
3. Leadership—Fiction. 4. Depressions—1929—Fiction.
5. Montana—History—20th century—Fiction.
6. United States—History—1933–1945—Fiction.] I. Title.
PZ7.I533Hi 2005
[Fic]—dc22 2004019447
ISBN-13: 978-0-15-204747-4 ISBN-10: 0-15-204747-6
ISBN-13: 978-0-15-205619-3 pb ISBN-10: 0-15-205619-X pb

Text set in Sabon
Designed by Kaelin Chappell

DOC 20 19 18 17
4500663924
Printed in the United States of America

For Troy and John

Although the events and characters in this book are fictional, they tell a story that was lived by many during the Great Depression. There was no Cold Day Camp or Civilian Conservation Corps Company 597 in Montana, but real CCC camps—4,500 of them, spread nationwide—provided homes, jobs, and training to three million enrollees, most of them like Moss and his buddies. These young men gave us replanted forests, restored rangeland and farmland, wildlife refuges, parks, monuments, and scenic lookouts. They faced tough times head-on and made something good of them.

Hitch

Part I

Part I

Chapter 1

I woke up shivering in the boxcar where I'd spent the night. Late October might be the tail end of summer in Texas, but it wasn't up here, wherever *here* was.

I coughed and ran my tongue over the grit clinging to my teeth. My body jangled with the vibration coming up from the train wheels.

Sharp lines of sunlight edged the wide, almost closed doors of the car and lay in stripes across the forms of men sprawled around me. *We must have passed out of the dust storm,* I thought, remembering the day before, when the train rushing north across farmland had entered a blackness of blowing dirt unlike anything I had ever seen.

First I'd wondered if the huge cloud moving toward us, too dark brown for rain, might be smoke. Then somebody called it for what it was, just before we got swallowed up in a violent torrent of sandpapering earth.

I'd fallen asleep to the howl of it.

Leaning into the boxcar door, I pushed it open. A wedge had kept it from shutting all the way—a safety against the bar-latch on the outside coming down and locking us in. Dazzlingly bright light flooded the car, and someone demanded, "You trying to blind us?"

"Sorry," I said, sliding the door far enough shut that the sunlight wasn't shining right on him.

He got up long enough to relieve himself against a wall, belch, scratch, and swear 'cause a bottle he picked up turned out empty. "Blind me again, kid," he said, "and I'll throw you under the wheels."

I turned away. That wasn't the worst I'd heard in the days since I left Muddy Springs and my job at the little Texas airport where I'd worked.

Days! It seemed more like weeks or months I'd been gone, like my last afternoon there happened in a different life even.

I closed my eyes to the endless country outside— butte and prairie land now, desolate looking—and saw again that scene I'd gone over and over. Lord, what a fool I'd been, playing at my job like I was some kid.

Dancing at it. *Dancing!*

"Come on, Miss McDonough! Hurry back!" I'd said aloud, swinging out my broom like it was my girl I was spinning across a dance floor. Of all the weekends for Beatty to be off to Dallas with her aunt and uncle. I had *news* to tell her.

I'd been accepted to radio school, and tuition was

even in a range I could afford if I watched every penny till next July when I could start. A thick letter from the school, along with a thinner one from my ma that I hadn't read yet, burned a hole in my back pocket.

Beatty and I, we had it planned. Come May—just another seven months—we'd be high school graduates, class of 1936. Then Beatty, who loved flying like she was born to it, would start flying full-time, for pay. She'd do contract work, like her teacher, Annie Boudreau, did. And I'd get serious about turning radios into more than a hobby.

I gave the broom another fancy turn. There wasn't anybody to see. The afternoon plane was long gone, and I had the Muddy Springs Airport terminal to myself. I just needed to finish sweeping, and then I could go up to my room and read all the radio-school pamphlets from start to finish.

"You always dance with brooms?" a man called out, and I whirled around, feeling like a right fool. I recognized one of the airport directors, a Mr. Kliber, that I knew by sight but no more.

"I'm 'feared you missed everybody," I told him. I explained how Grif—Beatty's uncle, who managed the airport—was away till Monday, and that his assistant had knocked off for the day.

"Actually, it's you I came to see," Mr. Kliber said. Puzzled, I said, "Yes, sir?"

"It's like this, Moss," he said, and commenced beating around the bush so bad I couldn't get what he was telling me. Then he finally said it straight out.

"You're firing me?" I asked. My voice sounded like it was coming out of somebody else's throat.

"I have to let you go," he said. "You can understand, Moss. The man we're hiring—I'll be honest, he's a cousin of mine—has a wife and children to take care of."

I nodded, feeling numb. I did understand. With Texas and the rest of the country deep in the Depression, a body had to understand favoring a family man over a teenager on his own.

It was just that I hadn't thought anybody else would want my part-time job, being the airport's janitor, mechanic's assistant, night watchman, and general gofer. I'd patched it together by pitching in wherever I'd seen a need. I got twelve dollars a week for doing it, and the room upstairs. Enough to live on, send some home to help my family, and save a bit.

I dragged my attention back to Mr. Kliber, who seemed bound to explain why his cousin had to have my job, now that he'd lost his own in a machine shop up in Oklahoma.

I broke in. "You needn't explain," I said. "I know how it is."

"You can have a couple days more," Mr. Kliber said. "I wish I didn't have to spring it on you this fast, but Orville's already on his way."

I went after a gum wrapper and dropped it into my dustpan, buying time to get control of the panic welling up. "I guess if I'm going, I best think about when to start," I said.

Maybe, I thought, as the train crossed a trestle, *that was where I went wrong.* For certain, I shouldn't have been so hasty to leave, shouldn't have let my pride get so wounded over being fired that I couldn't stay to face my friends.

I shouldn't have taken off without even leaving them a good-bye, telling myself I'd write when I had something proud to say.

But then there was that other letter, the one from my ma, in Spanish Creek, Louisiana.

Up in my bedroom above the terminal lobby, I'd read it. Now I took it out and read it again, the flimsy paper rattling in the wind.

Dear Son, she'd written, *I hope you are keeping well. I wished I could say we are but I am having a time making ends meet. We only did get money once from the WPA job I told you yr pa was on and then no more. I do not know if he is hurt or killed or taken off again without a say-so to anybody. If it is that he ought to be ashamed. Except for what you send, I would be at wits end caring for your brothers and sisters. But I don't complain, being just thankful the Lord gave me a good son. Yr loving mother, Bertha Trawnley.*

That hadn't left me any choice. Maybe I could have found a way to hang on in Muddy Springs myself, but there was no way I'd have gotten something that paid enough so that I could send Ma the help she needed.

The hobo in the corner swore at me again, but I

ignored him. The car reeked, so I wasn't about to close the door on anything less than another dust storm.

I'd lay money my father wasn't hurt or killed. He just wasn't doing his duty to his family like he ought. Just like he hadn't done it for a time now. Not since walking away from us two years ago. Not since before that, come down to it.

That last night in Muddy Springs I'd thought carefully about where my own duty lay and come up with a clear answer.

First I needed to mail my radio-school savings to Ma.

Then I needed to go find my pa at his WPA job in Montana and see he was all right. And if he *was,* then remind him he had a family to take care of. If I presented it careful, he'd realize he needed to send his wages home regular.

I wasn't sure what would come then. Maybe I could find some kind of job for myself up there, for the time being. Maybe I could even find some way to help him.

I'd packed my suitcase quickly—I didn't have much to put in it besides a few clothes, the letter from the radio school, and a picture of Beatty in front of an airplane. I left the next morning.

And now here I was, hundreds of miles from Texas. Well, one thing was for sure. I was more than ready to get to Montana and be done riding freight cars forever.

Chapter 2

My arrival into Miles City, on the state's eastern side, didn't go so good.

I went into the crowded train depot to ask directions to the Fort Peck Dam project, where Pa was working.

"There's a map on the wall," the ticket agent told me. "You're welcome to look, but make it snappy. I'm not supposed to allow loiterers."

Embarrassed, I made my way through the waiting passengers to where he'd pointed and then set down my suitcase. The map showed a whole tier of northern states, and I was just getting my bearings when the depot door opened and several fellows about my age came in. They were clean and slicked up, and each carried a grip of some kind. A couple had cardboard suitcases like mine.

Two or three of them nodded at me, and I nodded back but kept my attention on the map. I needed to get it figured before I got chased out. *Looks like I go due north. Fort Peck must be about a hundred miles.*

Someone tapped me on the shoulder, and I whirled around, grabbing up my bag, expecting to see the ticket agent. "I'm on my way," I said, before I saw it was one of the fellows who'd just come in.

He consulted a piece of paper. "Are you Bowman Bradley?" he asked. His nose was pinching in like he was trying to avoid smelling me.

"No," I answered. I'd never had anybody look at me like he was, and it made me hurry out from that place fast as I could go.

I was a hundred yards away when he came chasing after me, hollering that he wanted his suitcase.

"I don't have it!" I yelled back, but when I glanced down I saw I didn't have my own. The one I was carrying had wider stripes, and the handle was the wrong color.

"I'm sorry," I said, giving it over. "I must have picked up the wrong one."

"There's no other one inside," he said. "You were stealing mine."

"No!" I said.

But he was correct that my own suitcase wasn't anywhere in the depot. "Look," I told him, "I did have one. Someone else must have taken it."

"Sure," he said, "the one full of clean clothes. You think I'm stupid enough to believe that?"

"I wouldn't have come back to get it if—"

"You're just lucky I've got a schedule to keep to," he said, as a train pulled in. "Otherwise I'd file charges."

The waiting room had cleared before it really hit me that I'd just lost everything I wasn't wearing.

The agent said, "Guess you better go on now, son."

At a barbershop that offered use of a bathtub, I spent twenty of the fifty cents that was all the money I had left in my pocket.

Then, cleaner anyway, if not clean, I hit the road and put out my thumb. I slept in a hay shed and reached the construction town of Fort Peck, on the Missouri River, the next day. I asked around till I finally got directed to a personnel office in a building busy with guys hurrying in and out.

"I'm looking for my dad," I told a clerk. "Jackson Trawnley. He's got a job with the WPA."

"You're asking at the wrong office then," he said. "You need to go—"

A man in work clothes, wearing a hard hat, turned from a bulletin board he was reading. "Trawnley's gone," he said. "Left weeks ago."

"You know him, Red?" the clerk asked. "He was on your crew?"

"Nope, I wouldn't take him. Came in with a chip on his shoulder bigger than he was, asking for a job like it was the government's fault he needed it."

The clerk said, "Easy, now. This here's his kid."

"Well, I'm sorry," the one called Red said. "But I'm fed up with men who hire on and then don't want to work for anybody, or with anybody."

"But he *was* working here?" I asked. I had a bad-feeling knot growing in my stomach. "Did he get fired?"

"I don't know that," Red said. "But if you want to tag along a bit, I'll find you his foreman."

"Trawnley. Yeah, I had him," a young man told us, without taking his eyes off a six-man team reaching up to guide a huge metal wheel suspended from a crane.

"Easy out there!" he yelled. "Work together! Mind each other!" He didn't turn to Red and me till the piece was in place and the men all safely away from it.

"Now," he said, "Jackson Trawnley. No, I didn't fire him. I'd probably have had to sooner or later, but he saved me the trouble when he left."

"You mean he quit?" I asked, hoping I'd misunderstood. Maybe the man just meant my pa had transferred to someone else's crew.

"He blew up over an order I gave him, drew his month's pay, and lit out. Against regulations, but I wasn't sending anybody after him. Men that have to do everything their own way are a danger to everybody."

He hesitated before adding, "Same as men who don't control their drinking."

That distracted me. Made me hope, too, that perhaps he had Pa mixed up with somebody else. "My pa doesn't drink," I told him. "He never has held with liquor."

The older man, Red, the one who'd brought me out from the office, asked, "When was the last time you saw him?"

More than two years ago, when he walked off alone outside Muddy Springs, leaving the rest of us to fend for ourselves.

I asked Pa's foreman, "Do you know what he was going to do?"

"No idea. But I did hear he was headed to Miles City," he said. Then he added, "Look, you're not old enough for WPA work yourself, but you might find something at one of the rooming houses or eateries around here."

"I reckon I'll keep looking for my dad, like I set out to," I said. "Likely he's found other work by now. Maybe I can give him a hand."

"Good luck then," he told me.

As I walked off, I heard Red say, "I'm afraid that one's in for a disappointment."

Back in Miles City again, I tried the filling stations and automotive dealerships first, since machinery was the only thing Pa knew much about besides farming. Mostly I had no luck, although fellows at a couple of places said maybe my dad had been in.

"Wish I could be more help, but when you're not

hiring, you don't much notice who comes asking for a job," one told me.

Then I thought to ask at a place that sold farm equipment.

"Trawnley," the owner said. "Yeah, he came in here right on a day when, for once, I had more work than I could handle. I told him if he wanted to pitch in, I'd see how he did, and then we'd take it from there."

"So my dad's working for you?" I asked, hardly able to believe I'd found Pa so easy.

"No. He said he didn't need to prove himself to anybody, and that was that."

"Oh." I tried not to let on how disappointed I was. "I don't guess you know if he's still around?"

The man got busy polishing the grille on a tractor. "I might have seen him once or twice," he said. "You might want to check the bars come evening."

As I was about to go into yet another saloon, an unshaven man came shambling down the street. He reminded me of somebody, with his shoulders hunched and his old man's hair dirty and uncombed. I guessed I wouldn't have recognized him, but for he called out something to another fellow. I knew his voice.

"Pa?" I said. He didn't look over. "Jackson Trawnley?"

"Yeah?"

"It's me. Moss."

It took him a moment to process who I was, and

then there was another instant when his eyes shifted this way and that, like he was looking for an escape. But he said, "Well, what do you know! You are the last person I expected to see here!"

He sounded sober enough, but a whiff of alcohol hit my nose. He didn't smell none too clean, either.

"I came looking for you," I said. "Ma was worried when she didn't hear from you."

"Aw, she's a worrier," he told me, like it was some unwarranted peculiarity she had.

It made me mad. Actually, it felt right good to get mad, after the letdowns that had been jolting me one atop another.

"She's got a right to worry," I told him. "You disappeared for the longest. Then got her hopes up writing you had WPA work up here, only to disappear again. You know what she thought? She was scared you'd been hurt or killed. She should have known it was just you not holding a job."

"It wasn't a job. It was welfare. I told your ma the first time I tried relief work it wasn't for me. It demeaned me."

"And walking out on your family—and letting them down again—that didn't?"

I turned away in disgust but then turned back. "I don't know why I'm even surprised. Walking out's been your story all along, ever since our farm got sold.

"You could have hung on," I told him. "Uncle Lee said he'd take you on full-time in his shop, but no. You had to root us all up and head us to California. And when the trip got too much for Ma, you left her and us."

I caught myself up short, appalled by all the rage I'd thought was behind me. What Pa did two years ago wasn't the point now. Now I needed him to take hold and take back responsibility for our family.

Suddenly I knew who he'd reminded me of: all the men I'd ridden in boxcars with.

"Pa," I said, "what are you planning to do?"

"Oh, I'm biding my time," he said. "Looking around for where I might open my own garage."

"With what?" I asked, thinking I couldn't have heard right. "How are you going to pay rent? Buy tools?" His eyes were looking glazed. "Anyway, who'd hire a drunk to fix their cars?"

"I'm not a drunk," he said.

"You could have fooled me," I told him. "You stink of whisky, and you've got the trembles."

I stopped. He was looking whipped, like a dog getting hit every which way. Angry as I was, I hadn't meant to do that to him.

Then, he kind of gathered himself together, pulling bones up straighter and getting back a little of how he used to be, years before.

He said, "You get a civil tongue in your head before you come around me again."

As he walked off, I called, "Where are you going?"

He didn't answer, but I saw him duck into a saloon.

I considered following him and decided against it. All we'd do would be to argue more.

I slipped into a vacant lot across the street and settled down to wait, my back against a building.

I was already feeling terrible for disrespecting him the way I had.

And I was hating him for giving me a reason to.

Chapter 3

I pulled my jacket tighter around me, trying to ward off the night chill. I should have found out where Pa lived, so I could wait for him there. If he had a place.

Across the way, business at the bar had picked up for a couple of hours, and then the drinking crowd had begun thinning out again. I wondered when closing time was.

Finally, at what I guessed had to be after midnight, Pa stumbled out. I went over, prepared for the reek of his drinking, not expecting just how strong it would be.

"Come on," I said. "I'll get you home. Which way do we go?"

"Left," he answered. Half draped over me, he led us left again and again and once more. It brought us back to the saloon where we'd started.

A man, seeing us, said, "This that son you were talking about, Trawnley?"

"That's him," Pa answered, slurring his words bad.

I asked the man, "Do you know where my dad lives?"

"Doubt he has a place," the man answered. "But if you need a spot to put your head, there's a hobo camp sprung up a mile or so out of town. I doubt anyone will bother you there." He pointed to a side street. "That way. Just follow your nose till you see the campfires."

"Come on, Pa," I said, tugging on his arm.

He started around the side of the building.

"Where are you going?" I asked, following.

The alley he went into smelled of urine, and Pa couldn't get done adding to it fast enough to suit me. But then he sank down and curled into a ball.

"Hey, stand up," I told him. "We can't stay here."

I struggled to pull him to his feet, but he shook me off. "Leave me alone," he said. "I didn't ask you to come up here, telling me what to do." His speech was so garbled I had to think back on what I'd heard to understand it.

And then he was out cold, snoring loud.

I tried again to get him moving, but he was past waking. And skinny though he was, he was a dead-weight I couldn't budge. Finally I gave up trying. I just hoped we'd get through the night without freezing.

About dawn I was wakened by a foot prodding me. "You alive there?"

I looked up at a policeman.

"Yes, I am. We are. We're just—"

"There's a law against vagrancy."

"We're not vagrants. We're just—"

"Glad to hear it," he said. "'Cause I'd hate to have to run you in." A whistle sounded. "I suppose that's your train now?"

"What?" Pa asked, stirring. He looked from the policeman to me, seeming puzzled by the situation. His face cleared as it came to him who I was. "Moss!" he said. "What are you doing here?"

"Pa, we can talk later," I told him. "We've got to go."

I hauled him into a freight car, just glad the train had stopped. He was still too wobbly to have jumped.

I didn't even check to see which direction we were heading in till we were under way. The sun was rising behind us. We were going west.

Pa slept the morning off, while I tried to figure what we were going to do next. Not coming up with any bright answer, I finally gave up trying and contented myself with sitting in the boxcar doorway. The scenery wasn't all that different from the Dakotas. More crops to cattle, maybe, but mainly I saw worn-out land and signs everywhere of people struggling to make a living on it. Or the leavings where folks had given up trying.

I watched a man walking behind a mule team, plowing up crop stubble. Dust blew up around them.

"Fool!" Pa said, startling me. I hadn't heard him

come over. "Somebody ought to tell him farming's for fools."

"You didn't used to think so," I said. "We had a good place."

"Had. *Had!*"

"Couldn't you have done anything to keep it?" I asked. It was a question I'd never stopped wondering about.

"What?" Pa sounded defensive. "The one bank took my savings. The other waited for my cotton crop to fail and me to not pay my mortgage. They knew it was bound to happen, sometime."

He said, "Cotton's like that. Boll weevils one year. Not enough water the next. And the soil getting poorer all the time."

"So why didn't you try growing something different?"

"Because I was a cotton farmer! Why do you think? Like my pa and his. Our place always grew cotton."

I could see he wanted me to understand, but those weren't reasons!

"Maybe—" I broke off. I didn't have any *maybe* to offer. "Pa..."

He reached into a pocket and pulled out a whisky bottle. "Here."

"No," I said.

The railroad bulls got us early that afternoon, at a water-stop town at the far edge of another dust storm.

Likely it was the dirty haze hanging in the air that kept us from spotting the guards until they and their German shepherds were almost on us.

Maybe the hard-to-breathe filth was what made them ornery enough to haul us into jail, too, instead of just chasing us out of the boxcar with warnings and a few whacks of their batons.

Getting beaten would have shamed me, but nothing like being arrested did.

By the time Pa and I were in handcuffs, my heart was pounding hard enough to burst clear out of my chest. It didn't slow when we got taken to a little jailhouse, along with a couple of other hobos. We were booked for trespassing on railroad property and theft of transportation.

"Geez," said one of the men who'd got picked up with us. "And I thought we was just bumming rides." He told the officer he was John Smith.

The other man gave his name as Clark T. Gable. "That's with a *T*," he said. "Don't want you mixing me up with the movie star."

I mumbled my true one but didn't correct the officer when he wrote down Mose Tornley, and Pa didn't correct him over Jackson Tornley, either.

The four of us spent the night in a foul-smelling, concrete-block cell. Then the next morning we got hauled before a justice of the peace who let the men, including Pa, off for time served and a promise they'd leave town promptly.

The JP turned to me. "I'd like to keep you locked up awhile," he said. "Teach you a lesson while you're still young enough to learn it. But I can't do that without keeping your companions, and it isn't this town's job to feed no-goods."

I felt my face heat up, over being singled out as young and for the JP calling Pa and me worthless.

"As far as I'm concerned," he told Pa, "you're the worst of the lot, not doing more for your son than this. Well, take off! All of you. The next time you break the law, do it in someone else's jurisdiction."

We were going out the door when he called me back. "You! Tornley! The young one."

"Yes, sir?"

"Wait a minute," he said, as he hunted through a newspaper. He tore out a piece and motioned for me to take it. "Can you read?"

"Sure."

"Don't tell me 'sure.' Lots can't. Anyway, read that before you hop another freight train. It's about the CCC's fall enrollment. It's not too late to sign up."

Pa had followed me back in, and now he said, "CCC! Moss is too good for welfare and he knows it. Moss, you come with me."

"No, Moss, you wait," the JP said. "Before you leave I want you to take a hard look at your father. Is that how you want to turn out? Like him?"

Pa stalked off, and after a moment I followed.

No, I didn't want to turn out like him. Not like he

was now, anyway. But I didn't think the JP had any call to talk like he had. It wasn't right.

Heeding the JP's warning about his jurisdiction, Pa and I started walking north along a county road, aiming for a parallel branch of the railroad we'd come in on. As we walked, I tried talking about the newspaper article. "Maybe the CCC wouldn't be so bad," I said. "It would be a job anyway."

"Welfare," Pa said. "I told you, me and mine is done begging for government handouts."

"But if I was working, I wouldn't be begging."

"I told you, no!" he said, just before a trucker pulled up with an offer of a ride.

Finally we were on our way west again, and I was sitting in another boxcar doorway, my leg braced to steady myself against the constant jolt and sway, jolt and sway of the car passing over rail joints.

I held the newspaper clipping, though I about had it memorized. It didn't say much. Just that the CCC had openings for youths seventeen and older who wanted to do conservation work.

Pa had already told me to throw it away.

Just before, he'd pulled out a whisky bottle, which he'd somehow managed to find in the few moments we'd been in that last town.

Now he was out dead-cold drunk again, sleeping in a corner foul with other men's vomit. Geez. *Geez*.

Maybe if he'd been a stranger, I might have felt something besides the loathing that was fast replacing every other emotion. But he wasn't a stranger, who might have some excuse. He was my pa, who had brought this on himself.

No. That wasn't the all of it.

He'd brought this on his family. On my ma, who, soon as she learned I'd been fired, wouldn't know where to turn next.

Pa came to enough to grope around for the bottle and then dropped off again before his hand found it.

I couldn't blame him for me losing my job, but I could sure blame him for this...this...

I wrapped my arms around my head. What in the world was I going to do? Could I really do like the JP said, and turn out like my pa? That couldn't really happen, could it?

It was fear that it could, as much as anything, that made my decision for me.

I got off the train at the next good-sized town, without having got past Pa's drunken sleep to tell him good-bye. I found the town's name, Monroe, on a grain elevator.

Then I went looking for somebody to tell me where to sign up for the CCC.

Chapter 4

The postmistress directed me to the Monroe Hardware & Supply, which had a sign hanging from its locked door. BACK AT 4:00. Faded black lettering on a window announced OWEN SCHIELING, PROPRIETOR, and smaller, darker letters said CCC SELECTION AGENT.

I wiped away grime so I could read the small print of a taped-up leaflet, *A Chance to Work in the Forest*. It told how the Civilian Conservation Corps was carrying out conservation projects throughout the country—planting forests and restoring depleted farmland, building parks and wildlife refuges. That was as far as I'd got when a Model A pickup pulled up.

Its driver, a man maybe forty or so, wearing a fedora and tan jacket, got out with a broad smile of greeting. Unlocking the hardware store door, he said, "Sorry to keep you waiting. I got held up on some county business." He motioned me inside. "What can I do you for?"

"It's about the CCC," I said, nodding to let him know I'd caught his joke. "Are you who I need to see about joining up?"

"That's me! Selection Agent Owen Schieling! And I am glad to see you. You'll complete my quota."

He switched on a lightbulb above a scarred desk, lighting up a bit more of the long, narrow room with its floor-to-ceiling shelves and bins. "That's better," he said. "These gloomy afternoons—sure know winter's coming, don't we?"

He took some papers from a drawer, shuffled through them, and settled on one. "Now, where's my fountain pen? Ah! Okay, now! *Trawnley*. That's *T-r-a-w-n-l-e-y*?"

"Yes, sir."

"And *Moss*? What's that short for? Moseley?"

"No, sir. Just Moss."

"Oh. Right. And now where are you from?"

"Muddy Springs, Texas. Unless you want Louisiana. That's where I was born and grew up."

He looked over. "Can't put down either of those. Regulations say you enroll in your home state."

Dismay spread through me. "But…"

"Now, son, we can work it out. Why don't you tell me what brings you to Montana?"

"I came to join my dad," I answered. "I'd thought he was working up here, only he's not anymore."

"But he was, and now you've found your way here. Makes you downright local, far as I'm concerned."

Mr. Schieling wrote *Monroe, Mont.* on the form. "Now, you're seventeen?"

"On my last birthday, in May."

"Just a few more questions to qualify you. You unemployed?"

"Yes."

"Married?"

"No."

"Your family on public assistance?"

"No."

The selection agent tapped his pen. "Let's think about that. Technically they're supposed to be. The CCC program is for boys whose families need their help."

I hesitated. Despite all the reasons I had to be here, having to admit need shamed me, just like it had Pa. But Mr. Schieling was trying so hard to be helpful.

"Mine could use a hand," I admitted. "My mother's got all my brothers and sisters still to home and nothing coming in right now. I reckon they'd be on assistance; except where they live, there's not much relief money for anybody."

Schieling made another check. "The way I see it, my job's to put some common sense to the regulations."

Outside the window, a wagon came into view. A woman was driving it, and several kids were crammed into the back, tucked among furniture and bedsheet bundles. It reminded me of my own family, that time Pa made us move.

Our old, loaded-down car blew a tire on the highway outside Muddy Springs, which was how I ended up there. That's when Ma turned it around and took the littler ones back to Louisiana with her, Pa kept going on foot, and I stayed.

"That's Mrs. Morris," the selection agent said, glancing at the wagon. "She should have sold out a couple of years ago, instead of hanging on, piling up debts. But folks around here can be stubborn." He looked rueful. "Had to be from the start, to homestead dryland farms like her place, though, goodness knows, they got encouragement enough."

"Dryland farming?" I asked.

"No irrigation. It's possible when there's regular rain, but Montana saw the last of that back in '17. And by then the government and railroads had used promises of rich, free land to entice swarms of folk to move out here, half of them greenhorns who'd never spent a day of their lives in the country. *Dryland!* What they got was left high and dry when the drought hit."

His eyes briefly hardened with a look bitter as any I'd ever seen. "Took everybody else down with 'em, too, when they went broke," he said.

Then, just as quick, Mr. Schieling was all smiles again. "But a person's got to change with the times. When one thing doesn't work out, you find another, right Moss?"

"I guess. Yes, sir."

"Now, I'm supposed to ask what makes you want in the CCC."

"Mainly I just need a job," I said. "But while I was waiting for you I got to reading how the CCC wants to fix things. Restore the land and all. I don't rightly know how conservation's done, but I'll be proud to be in an outfit that's for it."

"Works for me," Mr. Schieling said.

"Sounds good to me, too."

I turned to see who'd spoken. An army officer was removing his hat. "I hope you're enrolling?" he asked me.

"We're just completing his application," Mr. Schieling said. "Moss, I'll need your mother's name and address, since most of your pay will be sent directly to her. It's a requirement of the program."

"I was going to send it anyways. She's Bertha Trawnley. She gets her mail at General Delivery, Spanish Creek, Louisiana."

I watched him write it down.

"Your initial period of service will be for six months, extendable for another six months." He turned the paper around and pointed to a line at the bottom. "Sign there. In doing so, you are swearing that the information you have given me is true, and you are authorizing the CCC to send twenty-five dollars of your monthly pay allotment of thirty dollars to your mother." He held out his pen.

I wrote my name while the two men watched.

"Welcome to the CCC, son," the army officer said.

"Your timing's good. A new group of enrollees starts conditioning camp at Fort Missoula this week."

I looked wildly at the paper I'd already handed back. Had I just joined the military?

The officer chuckled. "Don't worry. You're still a civilian. The army just trains the CCC's enrollees and runs its camps."

"I didn't know," I said.

"Now you do." He turned back to Mr. Schieling. "I stopped in to tell you the agreement's almost complete on that land where the new camp will go, and my staff will be getting in touch about buying provisions. I imagine you'll want to put in a bid to supply them?"

"For anything you need," Mr. Schieling said. "And meanwhile, I've been giving construction materials some thought." He reached for a file folder and then stopped himself.

"Almost forgot you, Moss!" Quickly filling in some lines on a voucher, he said, "This will get you a train ticket to Missoula. You can catch the 7:00 A.M. tomorrow." He gave me a leaflet. "And you might want to read this over."

"Thank you," I said and then added, addressing the officer, "and you, sir."

"I'm Major Garrett," he said. "I'm glad you signed on. I hope you'll make the most of the opportunities the CCC will give you."

Mr. Schieling followed me outside. "You have a place to stay tonight?" he asked.

"I'll find something," I told him.

He sorted through pocket change and handed me four bits. "This will get you a room," he said. "You'll see the hotel—the Monroe House—little two-story place down the street and around the corner from the Feed & Grain."

Chapter 5

I tossed and turned through the night, sick over how I'd betrayed my pa, and hoping the help I'd be giving Ma would make up for it.

Because it was a betrayal: throwing my lot in with an outfit he'd as good as ordered me to steer clear of.

Even if he didn't know. I hated thinking how, when he woke up, he must have wondered where I'd got to. It wouldn't have hurt to leave a note on him, saying.

As to worrying over what I'd got myself into, I did a fair amount of that, too. A six-month hitch seemed an endless stretch not to be able to return to Texas, no matter how much I got to missing Muddy Springs.

But sense returned with the dawn. My hitch would let me stop fretting over what to do with myself for the next half year, anyway, and it would mean steady money for Ma. Not a lot, but more than Pa would likely be sending her.

And Beatty would still be there when I got back.

———

The flapjack-and-egg breakfast that came with my room put me in better spirits, and when I headed for the train station, I reread the CCC leaflet as I walked.

Mostly it went into what I'd already learned about the CCC's mission, which I suspected sounded better on paper than put into practice. If the things wrong with the country could be fixed by a bunch of boys working together, then somebody would have fixed them by now.

The leaflet also included some parts I surely wished I could share with Beatty—especially the suggestions for items enrollees might want to bring with them: "a suit for excursions away from camp."

A suit! As if a fellow signing on for relief work would be likely to own one of those!

The list ended by saying, "If you play any small musical instrument such as a guitar, mandolin, ukulele, or harmonica, you are encouraged to bring it for use during recreational periods."

Maybe I'd hang on to the thing, and enclose it when I wrote her. *Beatty,* maybe I'd say, *would you be so good as to ship me my mandolin? I seemed to have forgotten to pack it.*

I enjoyed imagining how she'd laugh. We always found the same stuff funny.

I'd write her soon as I knew I'd be able to make a go of things.

I crossed to the depot, where a stocky guy already waited on the wooden platform. He wore town clothes—khaki pants and a pressed cotton shirt—but the band of pale skin at the top of his forehead gave him away as someone who spent his days outside, with a hat on. Ranch or farm kid, I guessed. A beat-up suitcase with a rope tied around it stood at his feet.

He glanced at the leaflet in my hand and asked, "You for the CCC?"

I said I was. "You?"

"Yeah. You got everything on that list?"

"Nope. Missing the mandolin. Someone was dreaming, huh?" I put out my hand. "I'm Moss Trawnley."

"Nate Lundgren."

A girl came running toward us, her coat flying open behind her in the morning's stiff breeze.

"My sister," Nate said, not sounding surprised. He yelled, "You can slow down! I'm not going anywhere in the next minute."

She reached us in a flurry of words. "I didn't want to miss you. I bought you a scarf. I got it sixty percent off because of damage, but it's warm."

"You didn't need to spend your money on me," Nate told her.

"Yes, I did," she said. "I ruined your old one."

"Ruined it mucking out the barnyard while I read. Maggie, this here's Moss Trawnley. Moss, my sister, who's got more mind of her own than a female ought."

"And it's a good thing for you I do," she told him.

I said, "I'm pleased to make your acquaintance, Miss Lundgren."

She raised her eyebrows. *"Miss?"* She echoed how I'd said it. *"Miz? Maggie* will do. Where are you from, Moss?"

"Texas. Louisiana before that."

"What brought your family up here? Or are you here by yourself?"

"Hey, hold up!" Nate told her. "You don't just give a guy the third degree."

"I'm not." Maggie's expression was half laugh and half apology. "At least I didn't mean to."

"I don't mind," I said.

The beep of a car horn interrupted us, and Mr. Schieling pulled up. "You boys remember your train vouchers?" he asked. He handed Nate and me each a box. "Your lunches. You'll be in camp for supper. Now you two do Monroe proud." He tipped his hat. "Maggie."

As he drove off, I said, "He seems like a nice fellow."

"He is," Nate replied, "although he owned a bank that went belly-up a few years back, and folks that lost money hold it against him."

Maggie said, "Sure they do, along with the people whose places he foreclosed on first. If he's nice, it's because he can afford to be, coming out with enough to open a business."

Nate shot her a disapproving look. "You shouldn't talk against him, Maggie. You need to understand the economics—"

"What I understand, Nate Lundgren, is that nothing you read in a book is going to keep people who've been hurt from being resentful. Aren't I right, Moss?"

Right as rain, I thought. I'd never forget the day my family's belongings went on the block, starting with the hundred acres that had been in my family for almost as many years. It was pretty land, spreading out around a low, dogtrot house with deep-shaded porches.

The auctioneer's gavel had knocked again and again, until almost everything my folks had owned was gone for less than what they owed.

"Moss," Maggie was saying, "I asked you, 'Aren't I right?'"

"I reckon," I said. "But I don't see much point in dwelling on what can't be helped." I lifted the lid on my lunch box. A powerful smell of freshly fried chicken wafted out. "And this is a nice meal Mr. Schieling gave us."

"*Gave,* my foot," Maggie said. "He'll get paid back."

"Sis, give it a rest!" Nate said. "You're going to have Moss thinking you are the most stubborn girl—"

"No," I answered quickly.

"Anyway, how'd you get off from the store?" Nate asked her. "Didn't you go in early for inventory?"

Maggie exclaimed, "Goodness! I forgot all about work." She gave her brother a quick peck on his cheek. "You take care, now, and you write about everything that goes on in that CCC. And don't worry about things at home. Moss, it was nice meeting you."

She rushed back down the street and disappeared into the mercantile, seeming to take the liveliest part of the morning with her. "She's got a job there?" I asked.

"Just a few hours on Saturdays," Nate told me. "She's still in high school—a senior, like I'd be if I hadn't had to stop going. We're twins."

A few minutes later, a westbound train came into view. "Guess this is ours," Nate said.

It stopped barely long enough for us to swing on board.

Chapter 6

Leaving Monroe, the train slid by grain silos and then picked up speed crossing land broken by deep-cut gullies and flat buttes. The view went on for miles, a patchwork of squared-off fields and fenced range. I saw a farmhouse next to the sod hut it must have replaced.

"Mr. Schieling was telling me about dryland farming," I said.

"Folks irrigate where they can, but the majority have to rely on rain," Nate said. "Or hope for it, anyway." He pointed out the window. "You can't quite see where I live, but it's out that way, a couple of miles west of town."

"You sorry to be leaving?" I asked.

"I'll be back. This CCC stuff is just temporary for me, to bring in a little cash."

A regretful look clouded his face, though he got rid of it quick enough. "What I'd really like to do is to go to the ag college in Bozeman and study how to run farms right. But that plan's on hold."

"I was aiming for radio-repair school," I said. "It's not going to happen anytime soon, either."

Then we didn't talk for a while more.

At first, looking out the window reminded me of looking out boxcar doors, when I was riding with Pa. With each mile that passed under me, though, and with each mile that took me closer to whatever was ahead, I thought less about him.

After crossing a wide swath of mountains, we pulled into Missoula in midafternoon. By then I'd walked the length of the train and spotted a few more boys who looked like CCC'ers. Still, I was surprised when, outside the Missoula train station, more than two dozen fellows gathered beside a big canvas-covered army truck where a uniformed soldier was bellowing, "CCC enrollees here! CCC, over here!"

The group mostly seemed about my age, though with a couple of older guys. And there was a younger kid, too, who I'd bet didn't even shave yet. He made me think there must be selection agents besides Mr. Schieling who stretched regulations some.

The soldier directed us to climb into the back of the truck and take seats on the benches that ran along each side of the flatbed. Looking around while trying not to seem nosy, I saw the others were doing the same.

It was easy to spot the poorest fellows: They carried paper sacks instead of suitcases. A guy who was wearing argyle socks and balancing a tennis racket drew second looks. I saw one guitar and any number of jackets as threadbare as my own. Everyone looked neat, though, with hair combed and faces clean.

And they looked like I felt: a little scared, now that the CCC was actually upon me.

Riding in a covered truck where you could only see out the back was like watching a movie being rewound: You left things behind instead of approaching them, and saw where you'd been, instead of where you were going.

I watched the train station and then Missoula's downtown disappear, and then neighborhoods of houses, and, across a river, a sawmill where a plume of smoke rose above a tall, cone-shaped furnace. "A tepee burner," somebody said. "For burning waste."

We were bouncing down a tree-lined road at Fort Missoula before I glimpsed the sentry we'd passed on duty at the post's entrance. By then, everyone on the truck was craning around, trying to see the big white billets, weedy fields, equipment yards, and long, low, wood buildings we were passing.

When the truck stopped, a soldier ordered, "Climb down! Make a line!"

He kept giving orders as we scrambled to obey. "I'm Sergeant Mackey. Make it a straight line, belongings

at your feet. You call me Sarge. We have a lot to do
between now and chow, so listen up. Leave your
things here while you get your physicals…"

What was left of the afternoon passed in a confusing
blur. Waiting my turn in a line that stretched out from
the infirmary's door, I again was reminded of watching a movie. Only this time, instead of unreeling backward, it seemed to be looping over and over, frames
showing one guy going inside and another coming out.
It was funny enough—I was imagining what Laurel
and Hardy could do with it, when my turn came.

First I was directed to a room where a bunch of us
were told to strip down to our underwear before
going out to a hall to wait some more. Dignity came
off with clothes, and it was worst for the fellows
whose skivvies had more holes than cloth.

And then waiting, clutching the medical record I'd
been told to hang on to, I sat next to a guy who was red
faced from strangling back a cough. Nodding toward a
room where guys were being called one at a time, he
asked me, "What do you think they do in there?"

"I'm guessing some doctor checks us over," I answered.

"You seen a doctor before?"

"Once or twice."

"I never have."

The army doctor eyed my leg bones and tapped
along my spine. "Asthma?" he asked. "Tuberculosis?

Hoof-and-mouth?" He laughed. "Just kidding, son. You look healthy enough to me, and for your reward, you get a round of inoculations, courtesy of Uncle Sam. Join the line in the next room."

Not everybody got the shots. The kid with the cough—he got a return ticket home instead.

When I finally emerged from the infirmary, both of my arms ached and I'd learned a joke I suspected I'd be hearing again: The CCC's just like the army, all hurry up and wait.

I'd also learned our enrollments weren't a sure thing after all. The CCC could send you home quick as it had taken you in.

And the long day still wasn't anywhere near over.

Sergeant Mackey had us stow our belongings in a barracks building that was filled with bare, narrow metal cots, each with a mattress rolled up on top. "Leave your gear and line up outside. That bugle you hear is calling you to formation."

We gathered at the flag in the middle of a big parade ground. While it was being lowered, soldiers saluted and ranks of CCC'ers further along in the program stood straight. Us first-day guys squared our shoulders and shuffled into a less ragged line, so's to make ourselves not stand out as newbies.

But of course everybody could see from our clothes we were, and, anyway, an officer walked out front next and welcomed us to Fort Missoula.

"You'll only be here for a couple of weeks before leaving for a work camp," he said, "but in that time you'll grow stronger from regular exercise and work. You'll learn what the CCC expects of you, and the CCC will have a chance to learn what you know and look you over. Make sure that what we see is good."

He studied us. "Some of you won't make it through these two weeks. Whether you will or won't is up to you."

Then he nodded to an enlisted soldier who hollered, "Dismissed!"

Most who'd been on post awhile streamed away toward what had to be a dining room, judging from the good smells coming from it. My group, uncertain if we were free to join them, stayed put.

Nate said, "The CCC's not getting rid of me, not now I've let 'em shoot me full of vaccines. Didn't you wonder what they were all for?"

"Typhoid, paratyphoid, and smallpox," answered the guy on Nate's other side. He was the one who'd brought the tennis racket. He was tall as me, but blond while I was towheaded. And with a different bearing. Like he was somebody.

"I inquired of one of the doctors," he said, as though he felt he had to explain knowing. He put out his hand. "I'm Sam Whitney."

Nate and I gave him our names, and then we had to be quiet because Sergeant Mackey was talking again, informally, introducing a guy wearing the denim work pants and jacket that seemed to be the CCC uniform.

Sergeant Mackey said, "This is Leader Reese. He and another junior leader will help you draw supplies and settle into your barracks later on, but right now he's going to get you some chow."

Someone said, "I'll be glad for that. I'm starved."

"You won't be for long," the sergeant said. "One thing about the army—and about any outfit the army runs—you can count on three hots and a cot." He chuckled at our puzzlement. "Three hot meals and a bed to sleep in." He turned to Reese. "They're yours," he said. "See you later."

Chapter 7

The mess hall was a large, open-raftered barn of a place, steamy warm with food smells, jammed with guys at long rows of tables. Reese led my group to some tables in one corner, and as soon as we sat down other CCC'ers began bringing us food: pitchers of milk; vast platters of meat loaf and sliced bread; bowls of green beans, mashed potatoes, gravy; dishes with butter and jam. Talk rose at other tables, jokes and laughter, but we sat in stunned silence.

So much food!

A thin guy seated opposite me wore an expression like he couldn't believe what he was seeing. "Holy moley! I didn't know anybody ate like this outside of the movies."

"You don't need permission to eat," Reese said. "Serve yourselves some of whatever's in front of you and pass it along."

The thin guy carefully put a small spoonful of potatoes on his plate and then, with a quick glance like he was afraid somebody would stop him, took a second, larger serving. And then up and down the table, others were doing the same thing. In minutes every one of us enrollees was digging into a plateful of food.

The meat loaf and all wasn't the end of it, either. Thick wedges of pie followed. A freckle-faced, friendly looking boy, lighting into a second or maybe third piece, kept saying between mouthfuls, "Ummm, ummmm, I mean to tell you. I do *mean* to tell you."

Finally Reese said, "Okay, listen up, everybody. Once Apple Pie down there is done eating, we'll head to quartermaster supply."

The freckle-faced kid waved good-naturedly. "Didn't want it to go to waste," he said, forking up a last bite of crust.

Getting supplied was bewildering as we tried to keep up with soldiers who were pulling items from bins and flinging them onto counters. I was given a roomy canvas bag that was supposed to hold everything: blue jeans and denim shirts, wool pants and wool shirts, underwear, socks, heavy shoes and overshoes, boots, work gloves, cap, heavy jacket. And then a razor, soap, metal soap box, metal mirror, toothbrush, toothpaste, and mess kit.

Nate, having as much trouble as I was fitting it all in, asked, "Why the mess kit? The mess hall had dishes."

"Son," one of the supply soldiers said, "I just give what the army says to give."

Another soldier added, "Because your next post might not have dishes, and maybe not a mess hall, either."

Loaded down, bumping each other with our armloads of new belongings, we finally returned to our barracks building, where someone had put sheets, two brown blankets, and a pillow beside each rolled-up mattress.

"Okay," Reese said. "Get your beds made and then put away your clothes and gear in the footlockers. Check mine over there in the corner to see how. Sarge'll be in at 2030 to look things over, and then 2130 is lights out. Questions?"

"What's 2030?" someone asked.

"Eight thirty," Reese answered. "You start counting hours at midnight and don't stop until you hit twenty-four. Other questions?"

"With all this we've done today, what's left for tomorrow?" someone else asked.

Reese grinned. "Sunday. A day of rest, which you'll be starting at 0545."

There was pause while that got processed, and then a disbelieving voice said, "That would be...5:45 A.M.? In the morning, 5:45 A.M.?"

A guy with slick-backed hair snickered. "We got us a genius."

The fellow who Reese had called Apple Pie flushed with embarrassment.

"All right, now. That's enough," Reese said. "Pick out bunks and get 'em made."

Nate, Sam, and I took our stuff to some beds in the middle, and I got to work trying to match the squared-off, tight blanket on Reese's cot. Nate, making lumpy bulges of his corners, complained, "I didn't plan on this. At home Maggie does all the bed making."

A boy across the aisle unfolded a sheet uncertainly, as though he was trying to figure out just what he held. It occurred to me that maybe the kid had never seen a bed made up with sheets before.

Sam, though, got his done perfectly in no time.

"Pretty good," I said. "Where'd you learn how?"

"Summer camp," he answered. "A long time ago. Back in Massachusetts." He flushed. "Guess that's more than you asked."

Others gave their names. The freckle-faced guy was Eddie Durgan, from Tennessee.

"And I thought your name was Apple!" Nate said.

The barracks door opened, and Reese called, "Hey, everybody! Here's your other junior leader. Anybody having bed-making troubles, just take them to Bill Compton."

I looked and then looked again, and my heart sank. It was the guy I'd had the run-in with back in Miles City. The one who thought I'd stolen his suitcase.

He didn't seem to like how Reese had introduced him. He gave this stiff-necked nod of acknowledgment as his gaze swept across us. I was relieved when it had passed by with no sign he'd recognized me.

I turned back to the work at hand and to the fellows I was getting to know.

Already guys were splitting into groups as we milled around, unpacking, going back and forth to see how Reese's footlocker was arranged.

Of course some fellows had arrived already knowing each other. There was a good number that hailed from various parts of Montana, and a half-dozen Carolina guys who'd arrived on the same train with Eddie Durgan—or Apple, as everyone already called him.

The guy who'd hassled him about the time was one of a pair. He kept with another who spoke in the same fast, sharp, Yankee accent. "The Bronx," one of them answered shortly, when someone asked where they were from, "if it's any of your business."

Rudelike, but I likely wouldn't have marked them 'specially, except that I accidentally kicked over some clothes one of them had piled on the floor.

The guy who'd said he was from the Bronx was in my face in an instant, acting like I'd done it on purpose. "Pick 'em up," he said. "And fold 'em while you're at it." He jabbed at my shoulder.

I jabbed back. "Knock it off!" I said. "I'm sorry I kicked your stuff, but you got no cause—"

He jabbed harder, and this time I hit his arm away.

"Back off!" a voice commanded. "Now!" Compton stepped between us, shoving us apart. "What are your names?"

"Klein," the guy muttered in a sullen voice.

"That's it?"

"Joe Klein."

"Moss Trawnley," I answered.

"This incident will be noted. Consider yourselves warned. Fighting is not tolerated. Is that understood?"

He got a grudging nod from Klein, and I said, "Yes."

"All right then," Compton said, his gaze on me suddenly intent. "Haven't I see you someplace before?" His expression sharpened. "I did. In the Miles City depot the other day. You took my bag."

"No, I—"

Reese came over just then. "Is there a problem?"

Compton's eyes locked on mine. "There'd better not be," he said. "I'll be watching you extra close, Trawnley."

"What was that all about?" Nate asked.

"A misunderstanding," I answered. "Compton and me got off on the wrong foot."

"It'll blow over," Sam said. "Or, if it doesn't, at least you can say good-bye to him when we leave for work camp."

I didn't answer. I wasn't used to practical strangers asking about my problems or commenting on them.

All around, talk was growing louder and more familiar as guys finished squaring away their areas. Facts about who people were came at me faster than I could remember them. Four guys with Polish names were from Butte, signed onto the CCC because their fathers had lost jobs in the copper mines. A guy from Pennsylvania said it was the same thing with him, only it was a steel mill job that his pop had got laid off from.

Compton had to call us to order twice before everybody heard that the sergeant was on his way in.

Sergeant Mackey took one look at the beds, not any two of them made up the same way, and just shook his head.

Forty-five minutes later—after the junior leaders had us make and remake our beds till we'd got them close to right—Reese finally said it was time to knock off. "You've got fifteen minutes until lights-out at 2130. Be in your bunks when they do."

His last words got drowned out in the stampede to the latrine.

I'd done all right up till then, I thought, or at least I'd done as well as anybody had getting through the confusing day. Not counting the dustup with Klein and Compton, of course.

But waiting for my turn at one of the sinks, jostled by guys on both sides, it suddenly hit me how this was going to be my life for the next six months. How, from now on, I was going to be doing everything in a group. Sleeping, eating, working. Even brushing my teeth.

Had it really been just that morning that I'd waked up in the Monroe House, still a guy on my lonesome?

I had to clamp down every leg muscle to keep from bolting.

When I finally reached a sink, I dawdled while the latrine emptied, till I had the place to myself. For the first time in hours I didn't have somebody within two feet of my elbow.

The door opened, and Compton stuck his head in. "Enrollee, you're—" he began, as I turned. "Trawnley!"

He looked provoked, and I expected sharp words. But then Reese came in and said, friendly enough, "You're going to have to find your bunk in the dark, enrollee, since you just missed lights-out."

"I didn't mean to," I said. "I'm sorry."

Compton got the last word. "Apologies don't cut it, Trawnley. Do things right from now on."

Chapter 8

"Church services are voluntary," Reese said the next morning, after we'd stumbled through an unfamiliar schedule of barracks tidying and formation and another mess hall meal. "Everybody line up."

After that there was a big dinner, and then Reese told us, "The afternoon's yours. You can go where you want, as long as you stay on post. There's a recreation hall, lots of places for a ball game—"

"Can we just sleep?" someone asked.

"If you want. You won't have ten minutes for a nap after today."

Sam and Nate wanted to go exploring.

"You guys go on," I told him. "I need to write a couple of letters."

Apple went with me to the rec hall, where we settled at a table equipped with stationery and envelopes, even fountain pens and a bottle of ink. The place was pretty quiet, just some fellows playing Ping-Pong and a few reading magazines. Compton and another junior leader were talking over Coca-Colas, but they didn't pay us any mind.

Dear Ma, I began my first letter, *Well, I am in the CCC. I saw Pa and he is not hurt, but he has now moved on. I hope you will hear from him soon. Meanwhile, the CCC will send you most of my pay, so you'll have that besides what I sent earlier.*

Say hi to the kids for me and tell them I said help you some. I am all right. Love, Moss.

P.S. I am at an army post named Fort Missoula for a short time. When I get to a regular work camp, I will send you my address.

Writing Beatty was a different chore altogether. Once I got *Dear Beatty* down, I was stuck. I owed her—and her aunt and uncle and just about everybody I knew in Muddy Springs—an apology for taking off without saying good-bye or leaving word where I was going.

But I couldn't figure out how to write it without sounding like I wanted them to be sorry for me, or like I was expecting their help.

I guess I must have made some sound, because Apple said, "Tough going?"

"Yeah. I need to right a wrong with my girl, and I don't know how to start."

"Can't help you," he said. "I've never had a girlfriend, though I got hopes. This here's to my folks, 'cause my mother made me promise I'd write regular. She said the CCC couldn't have me otherwise."

I laughed. "She sounds like a nice mom."

"Yeah. And Tennessee's a long way away."

I read over what I'd written so far—*Dear Beatty*—and added *How are you? I am fine.*

I crossed out *fine*. I didn't want her thinking I thought things were too good, when I was away up here and her down there. I wondered if I should apologize up front or work into it, after doing some explaining.

Then Apple startled me, exclaiming "Hey!" as his pen skidded across the desk, spilling blue ink.

"Sorry!" It was Klein. He and his buddy, Colie Lukowski, were right behind Apple. Klein's *sorry* didn't sound at all like he meant it.

"What'd you hit me for?" Apple said. "You made me mess up my letter."

"Oh no! Which one is it?" Klein said, snatching up both Apple's and mine.

"Give them back!" Apple said, as he and I stood. He was all set to pitch into a fight. That was the last thing we needed.

I stepped between him and Klein, hoping to prevent one. "Now!" I said, putting out my hand. "Both of them."

"Or you're gonna make me?" Klein mocked, pretending to be frightened. He was putting on for his friend's benefit, and Lukowski was eating it up. "Hillbilly here's trying to scare us. What are we going to do?"

He started to pull the letters out of reach, and I grabbed his arm. He jerked back, and...

Whatever would have happened next between us didn't, because Compton was suddenly on us, demanding, "What's going on?"

Klein dropped the pages so they floated to the floor. "Nothing," he said. "We was just joking around."

"Then after this, keep the horseplay outdoors."

Compton looked from one to the other of us, his eyes settling on me. "I don't think you much want to make it here, Trawnley."

Monday began the workweek routine, and for the next few days, everyone, including me, was flat out too busy to get into trouble.

The 0545 wake-up was followed by reveille bugled to the tune of *"You can't get 'em up, you can't get 'em up, you can't get 'em up in the mornin'*," only Reese and Compton did get us up and outside in time for calisthenics at 0600. And then there was washing and dressing, straightening the quarters and breakfast, formation and assignments at 0800, and then a long day of work projects Sergeant Mackey said were planned to "strength, toughen, and test."

Or wear us out.

Monday, when we knocked off work at 4:30 P.M.— 1630, according to the army and the CCC—we pretty much collapsed till call to colors.

Tuesday, though, a few rallied for a softball game,

and by Wednesday we'd chosen up semipermanent teams. Sam turned out to be a pretty good pitcher, and I played shortstop. It was a rousing good game that ended when Nate batted a home run with two runners on base. It gave our side a victory that we celebrated loudly, and Apple, who was playing outfield for the other side, flashed him a thumbs-up.

Thursday we took our first long hike. "We're going to get you in shape to put in eight healthy hours a day in the outdoors," Sergeant Mackey told us, as we got ready. "Because when you leave here, most of you will be going to outside jobs, planting trees or clearing weeds, building parks."

"Do we get to choose?" someone asked.

The sergeant laughed. "Nope."

"But we won't be split up?" Apple asked. "We'll all go to the same place?"

"That's right. Now, you wouldn't be asking all these questions just to put off a little walking, would you?"

We did ten miles, getting back in time for lunch and an afternoon of learning to use axes. We thinned out a stand of spindly pines on the post's perimeter.

Apple, still speculating about our assignments, said, "Where I really want to go is Yellowstone Park. I hear there's so many CCC'ers there, they've got all kinds of stuff going on like boxing matches and fishing contests. And I wouldn't mind seeing those geysers. Maybe get my picture taken next to Old Faithful, and then go inside that big hotel they got there and treat myself to a fine meal. You think—"

"I think," Sam said, "you better pay attention to what you're doing, before you chop off your foot."

"Aw," Apple said, "I learned to use an ax about the time I got baby teeth."

"I wish I had," Sam said. It was as close as he'd come to complaining, though several popped blisters had made the palms of his hands sore things to look at.

His tennis racket had disappeared, but other stuff, like the blisters and his educated way of talking, set him apart from most of us. Whenever he got asked why he'd joined the CCC, though, he'd just joke, "Why, I came to fix the country's dust bowl."

It was more restraint than most showed.

I couldn't get used to people making free with personal business. It was impossible not to hear this or that about where guys came from, or why they'd joined up.

Workwise, several fellows were like Nate and Apple and me, come to the CCC already knowing how to use shovels and picks, and with the calluses to prove it. More than one of them told about some hardship farm.

Others, like Klein and Lukowski, were city smart in a sharp, take-care-of-yourself kind of way, and some of the things they threw out about gang fights and tenement rats were enough to make your hair curl. Most of the city fellows got friendly soon enough, though. Just Klein and Lukowski stayed as disagreeable as a couple of boils on your behind.

Compton was the other pain, bent on turning us

into a shipshape outfit or knowing the reason why. It was always *Make that bed again, Enrollee Lundgren!* or *Enrollee Durgan! Tuck in your shirt!*

He had it in for Klein and Lukowski, especially after Klein bragged on how they were only in the CCC because of being picked up on shoplifting charges. A judge had let them choose between juvenile detention and joining up.

"The CCC is not supposed to be a substitute for jail," Compton said.

And of course he had it in for me, and for Sam, Nate, and Apple, on account of they were my friends. I apologized for the way Compton was hassling them because of me.

Nate, easygoing, said he hadn't noticed.

Apple was all for dealing with Compton as a group. "That's the only way," he said. "Hit him with an overwhelming force! We could...could..."

He laughed at himself. "When I think of something good, I'll let you know."

Sam said, "We're only here another week and a half. The prudent course will be to avoid crossing him."

"Amen to that," I said.

Chapter 9

I should have tried harder to take Sam's advice, which exactly matched what I'd decided for myself, anyway. I meant to avoid crossing Compton, and I would have, if Klein and Lukowski had played fair with Apple when the three of them got assigned to work together.

After the first night, mess hall duties were rotated among the guys in our barracks. Each day some of us got put on one of the details there: table setting, serving, or cleaning up. On the Thursday of that first long hike, Apple drew evening cleanup, along with Klein and Lukowski.

Thursday was movie night in the camp, and most of the rest of us went to see a film about the national parks. The National Park Service used a lot of CCC'ers.

It didn't last long, and the newsreel that followed— mainly about the new Social Security Act to take care of old people—didn't either. When the lights came back on I was surprised to see Klein and Lukowski there. I wouldn't have thought they could finish the kitchen work so fast.

Apple wasn't in sight, though, and he wasn't in the barracks, either, when we went back there.

"What do you think he's doing?" Sam said.

"Probably found tomorrow's desserts and started eating," Nate guessed.

Apple tore in after taps, with bare seconds to spare before Compton and Reese would do a bed check.

"Where have you been?" I whispered, but Apple didn't answer.

It wasn't till calisthenics the next morning that we got the story out of him, told in huffs and puffs between sit-ups and jumping jacks.

Klein and Lukowski had stayed on cleanup with him only until the last of the kitchen staff had left. Then they'd taken off, leaving him with a mound of pots and pans still to do.

"And you didn't stop them?" Nate asked, sounding disbelieving.

"I started after them. But then I got to thinking: what if the mess hall sergeant came back and found us all gone? He'd think I'd skipped out, too." Apple groaned his relief as the last sit-up was counted.

"They had no business leaving you to do your work and theirs both," Nate said. "You should have reported them."

"I almost did," Apple said. "But then I got thinking that if I was taken advantage of, it was my own fault for letting it happen. And, besides, telling on them... it wouldn't be right."

"Why not?" Nate demanded.

Apple seemed lost for an explanation.

Sam said, "I think I understand. On the one hand, reporting Klein and Lukowski would have been giving up one's peers, which is not done. But on the other—"

"You talk like a lawyer," Nate interrupted, while watching to see what exercise we were doing next.

"I'm only articulating what—" Sam broke off, looking embarrassed. "I do, don't I?"

"Or a politician," Nate said. "A senator. That's what we should call you. The Senator."

"So now," Apple said, looking glad to have the attention turned off him, "somebody besides me's got a nickname. Who gets one next? Moss?"

Nate and Sam both started to say something they thought better of. Probably that *Moss,* itself, was as good as a nickname.

Nate got serious again. "Really, Apple, you have to stand up for yourself."

Apple, struggling to touch his toes without bending his knees, said, "I know. I should have pitched into them when I had the chance. Next time I will."

"You mean that?" I asked him, as we walked to breakfast.

"Sure," he said. "You know the saying. 'Fool me once, shame on you. Fool me twice, shame on me.'"

"But you're not going to do anything hotheaded? Everybody's been warned about fighting, and Compton's already got you and me marked from that business Sunday."

"Stop worrying," Apple said. "With luck I won't have to work with those two again, anyway."

I hoped not, because I liked Apple, and I didn't want to see him pitched out of the CCC for being a troublemaker.

Nate was right. The only way to deal with guys like Klein and Lukowski was to stand up to them. But there were ways to do it that didn't start with throwing a punch, which I feared would be Apple's way.

When work details got assigned that day, I got trash burning, Sam and Nate were put on grounds cleanup— that meant picking up cigarette butts—and Apple, Klein, and Lukowski drew the latrines.

That detail always caused a laugh and some crude jokes because of the nature of it, and the guys on it were expected to make snappy comebacks. Klein and Lukowski, though, just glowered. And I could see Apple gearing up for something.

Before I could stop myself, I was asking him, "Say, you want to switch? I'd rather swab out showers than sweat over a fire."

"No, you wouldn't," he said.

"Really," I said. "Anyway, you can switch with me the next time I draw KP. Peeling a barrel of potatoes like I did the other day—that's one job I don't ever want again."

"They're just going to try to walk all over you like they did me."

"I won't let them," I promised. "I won't give them a chance."

I read down the chores list posted on the latrine closet where the brushes and mops were kept. "We've got to scrub showers, toilets, and sinks. Also mop the floor. What do you guys want to start with?"

Not getting an answer, I repeated the question. "I said, what jobs do you want?"

"I think just watching you work will be job enough," Klein said, and Lukowski snickered.

"No, it won't," I said. I threw Lukowski a can of scouring powder that he had to catch to avoid getting hit by it. "You can do sinks."

Then I told Klein, who was leaning against a wall, "That leaves johns and showers. Take your pick."

"I ain't picking nothing," Klein said, pulling out a cigarette and lighting it.

"Then I'll do the showers. Here!" I tossed a toilet brush to him.

Klein swore, caught it, and flung it back.

I let it fall. "Up to you," I said, starting toward the showers. I'd do my part, but no more, and I'd leave it to him to explain why the whole latrine wasn't finished proper.

He moved in quick as a rattlesnake strikes, and before I knew how it happened, we were on the floor fighting.

I was struggling to get a solid hold on him when he landed a blow that cracked hard under my cheekbone. Blood stung my eye as I hit back.

Lukowski's voice broke through the ringing in my ears. "Someone's coming."

We scrambled up, but Klein wasn't near done. He shoved me again, and I shoved back. We crashed sideways, knocking loose a tall pipe that crashed into a toilet bowl, shattering it. Water was cascading everywhere when the latrine door opened.

Sergeant Mackey moved in fast, and Compton was right behind him. The sergeant splashed through the spreading water to turn a shutoff value before ordering, "Get on your feet. Clean this mess up and then report to the company commander's office."

"Shall I remain with them?" Compton asked.

"No."

For several moments there was just the sound of their footsteps growing fainter.

Then Klein said, "The hell with this"—and started out—"You coming, Lukowski?"

Lukowski said, "Don't you think—"

"Think what? That Captain Strom's going to say, 'You did such a good job cleaning up; you're forgiven'?"

"No, but—"

"We're going to get thrown out. Even dumb Trawnley there knows that, don't you Moss? Thrown out on your hillbilly ear."

Lukowski said, "But—"

Klein snorted. "Be a sucker if you want. I'm gone." And then he did leave, and soon after, Lukowski followed him.

Klein was right, I thought. We were out.

But I got a mop from the closet, anyway, and I began sopping up the water that was as deep as the soles of my shoes.

Chapter 10

I worked till that latrine sparkled, all the while picturing what must be going on in the captain's office: Sergeant Mackey making his report and the CO's reaction. I wondered if they'd already got my dismissal papers written up and a railroad pass made out to return me to...Return me where? I guessed to Monroe, where I'd signed on.

I didn't let myself think past that, to what I'd do then.

Finally, when there wasn't a surface left to clean and it was still just ten thirty in the morning, I put away the brushes and mop and started for the headquarters building.

Some CCC'ers were coming in from a hike, shouting out the last verses to a song, and I knew how good they felt stretching their legs and lungs.

Across the parade ground another gang of guys in CCC denim were unloading lumber from a truck. I guessed they were starting on the review platform Sergeant Mackey had said we'd be working on, to learn tools.

I smelled onions and beef cooking and wished I hadn't been so fast to think I could handle Klein and Lukowski better than Apple could. If I hadn't, I'd be eating stew with my buddies, come lunchtime.

It was a hard thing to get my mind around—how I'd been part of it all and now wouldn't be, and just when I was getting to like it.

It was hard to think how things here would be going on the same way come tomorrow and the next day, but all without me.

I hesitated outside Captain Strom's office, thought *Might as well get this over,* and went in. "I'm Moss Trawnley," I told the first soldier I saw. "Sergeant Mackey said I should report here."

"You took your time showing up. Where are the others?"

"I don't know."

The soldier frowned and told me, "Well, you're going to have to wait to get your discharges signed. The CO's late getting back from a trip." He pointed to a bench. "Over there."

When Captain Strom still hadn't returned by quarter of twelve, the orderly told me to rejoin my outfit for the noon meal and then report back afterward.

I cut across the parade ground and angled by a row

of young trees. Down at the far end, a buck deer had pulled loose a wire protective cage and was rubbing his antlers on the tree trunk.

He's going to kill it, I thought, remembering how we used to girdle weed trees back home. With a ring of bark gone, a tree couldn't pull up water and minerals.

I shouted to scare him off, and when I went by the tree, I looked to see what damage he'd done. Not much, yet. I replaced the cage and twisted some fastening wires tight before going on.

I saw a pair of officers some distance away watching me. I thought I recognized Major Garrett, from Mr. Schieling's hardware store in Monroe. I wasn't sure, though. The other man was talking and shaking his head.

Then I saw my outfit come jogging up from another direction and disappear into the barracks. I went after them, dragging my steps. Sam and Nate and Apple probably already knew about the fight—likely everybody did, gossip traveling fast—and they'd be waiting for me.

Only, nobody *was* waiting for me in the barracks, which was in an uproar. Fellows were tearing through their footlockers, and cries of "My money's gone!" and "I had five dollars!" and "My watch! It was hid good in my socks..." were sounding all around.

Everybody had to wait while some military staff investigated, and we almost missed lunch. Because I'd been separated from the others most of the morning, I came in for extra questioning, but it was pretty clear to everybody that Klein and Lukowski were responsible for the thefts. Their belongings were gone, and no one remembered seeing them after they'd left me alone in the latrine.

I caught some angry looks, but Nate said, "Don't let it get to you. Guys have got to be mad at somebody right now. It may take a couple of days, but once they calm down, they'll realize you couldn't help what those two did."

"Sure," I said. "Only I'm not going to be here then. I'll be leaving as soon as Captain Strom gets back and makes my discharge official."

"No!" Sam protested.

"I don't believe that," Apple said.

"That's really tough," Nate said. "I'm sorry, Moss."

I didn't want anybody feeling sorry for me, so I went for a joke. "I'll remember you galoots," I said. "And I'll be watching the news, too. If the country's dust bowl isn't fixed by the time your hitches are up, I'll know you slacked off on the job."

The CO still hadn't returned by the end of the afternoon. "You want him for the night?" the desk clerk asked Sergeant Mackey, when the sergeant came in at quitting time.

"No, but I guess I've got no choice," he said. He told me, "Consider yourself confined to barracks, except for what's on the company schedule, until you're called."

I listened to Nate snoring and to Sam muttering in some dream. I was going to miss them and Apple, even if they were forgetting me mighty fast. Otherwise, they'd have kept me company through the evening, instead of going off to the recreation hall.

They'd been a disappointment, no two ways about that.

Though not as big a disappointment as I'd been to myself. If I couldn't sleep, it was because I was too angry about messing up like I did. I should have just cleaned the danged latrine. One morning's work. It wouldn't have killed me. It hadn't when I'd ended up cleaning the whole thing, anyway.

I was still awake when reveille sounded the next morning, and I couldn't help regretting that it was the last time I'd hear it.

And even though I knew wishing was useless, I sure wished I'd get another chance to do things right.

Chapter 11

"You heard anything?" Nate asked, as the company gathered for morning formation.

"No. Not yet." A scene from an army movie popped into my mind, a whole company of cavalry-men watching the stripes being torn from the shirt of a soldier who was being thrown out. *Cashiered.* That was the word.

They wouldn't do that here, would they? Dismiss me in front of the whole company, so everybody would see my disgrace?

The flag got raised. Sergeant Mackey told about the day's schedule. Since it was Saturday, guys would get some time off. Then the CO took over, something not usual in the morning, and I felt a clammy sweat break out on my hands.

"A couple of things, men," Captain Strom began. "First, I want to encourage any of you who missed the movie on the national parks to see the rerun of it this evening. And pay special attention to the part about the Grand Canyon."

He paused, smiling at a ripple of excited murmurs. "That's right. Assignments have come through. That's where most of you are headed."

Yahoos broke out up and down the line.

"Now though," he continued, "I'm going to turn things over to Major Garrett, who's got different plans for a small group of you."

The major, who I hadn't noticed standing off to one side, now stepped forward. He looked over the company, his eyes stopping on me a moment.

"The Grand Canyon's a great assignment," he said, "but I can offer a pretty good alternative. I've been charged with establishing a new CCC camp here in Montana, near Monroe, on the other side of the mountains."

I heard Nate draw in his breath.

The major continued. "It will be under the auspices of the Soil Conservation Service, and it's going to be tackling a variety of projects that will help that area turn itself around and bring land back into production.

"Right now the camp is just a bare field, though, and that's why I'm here. I'm to pick a construction cadre to leave with me today, to begin putting up the buildings needed to house yourselves plus the additional one hundred forty enrollees who will be arriving in less than six weeks."

He paused to let that sink in.

"So," he went on, "I'm looking for eighteen volunteers who'll put in the next month and a half working harder than you've ever worked. In return, you'll learn a variety of construction skills and you'll get to stay on here in Montana as a member of a brand-new camp with an important mission.

"I'm requesting a few individuals for various reasons. Linchfeld, you've had some building experience. Lundgren, I'm assuming you'll want in, since your family's in Monroe. Moss Trawnley, we can use some mechanic's skills. Now, that leaves fifteen slots. Volunteers?"

Talk broke out, but I didn't listen.

I was going? They were letting me stay in after all? I wanted to shout out a huge *Yes!*

Then a different thought sent my spirits plunging. What if Captain Strom just hadn't heard about the latrine fight yet, and once he did, I'd be taken off Major Garrett's list and discharged after all?

Hands were going up here and there, mostly Montana boys wanting to stay in state.

I heard Sam say, "Samuel Whitney, sir. I'd like to volunteer."

"Very good. That makes seventeen. I need one more."

And then Apple muttered, sounding anguished, "The Grand Canyon! I don't believe it. That's as good as Yellowstone! What a guy doesn't have to do for his buddies."

He raised his hand, "Edward Durgan," he said. "I'll go."

"That's the group, then," the major said. "I'd like to talk to you for a few moments before breakfast."

Sergeant Mackey took over. "You heard it. Construction cadre stay here. The rest of you, dismissed!"

The formation broke up amid loud chatter. My friends slapped my back.

"See!" Nate said. "I told you!"

"If it's not a mistake," I said.

"All right," Major Garrett said. "Gather around. I'm going to make this fast, because I want you to get some food in you and then get your belongings packed up fast. A truck will pick you up at 0900 to take you to the railroad station. I'll fill you in more once we're on our way, but does anyone have any immediate questions?"

One of the Montana enrollees said, "I'm just wondering, are we supposed to build the camp all by ourselves?"

"You'll be working with local carpenters, and the army has developed construction procedures that are fast and simple."

Sam asked, "What about the rest of our conditioning period here?"

"It's over as of now." Major Garrett glanced around. "Okay. If that's it, you better get yourselves to the mess hall."

I turned to my friends. "You guys go on to breakfast," I told them. "I'll catch up."

I waited until there were just me and the major left. "Sir, I want to thank you for choosing me," I said. "But, I was wondering...That is, I got into some trouble yesterday, and I was kind of thinking—"

"I heard about it," Major Garrett said. "I have to tell you that if anything like it happens again, you'll be out of the CCC so fast you won't know what happened."

"But I'm not now?"

"No."

"Then I guess I need to thank you for giving me a second chance," I said.

Major Garrett shook his head. "That was your company commander's decision. I just suggested that if you were to be allowed to stay on, the Monroe camp might be a good assignment for you."

"I see," I said, though I didn't, really. "Well, anyway, thank you."

"As I said, you're thanking the wrong man."

I skipped breakfast so I'd be waiting outside Captain Strom's office when he got there.

"Sir," I said, "I'm Enrollee Moss Trawnley—"

"I know who you are."

"Major Garrett said you're letting me stay in, despite

yesterday, and I wanted to say I'm grateful. Also, that I'm sorry for what happened."

"You came within a hairsbreadth of being thrown out. And you're going to have to make good on the broken fixture. A replacement's going to cost the corps around seven dollars, and that's money you won't see come payday."

"I don't mind, sir," I said.

"Since the other two are gone, you're going to have to pay it all yourself."

"I understand. I will."

"Frankly, my first inclination *was* to get rid of you. The CCC doesn't need hotheads causing dissension and maybe giving the communities where we put our camps a reason not to welcome us. But I respect what others say, and you certainly had a lot of people going to bat for you. Sergeant Mackey, especially."

"The sergeant?" I asked. "He was on my side?"

"He said you didn't make excuses for yourself. And that you finished the job you'd been given, despite the other two skipping out. That showed character.

"Though, of course, you should have gone to your junior leaders when the trouble with Klein and Lukowski first started, instead of taking matters into your own hands. If your friends hadn't explained things to Leader Reese last evening and gone with him to track down Sergeant Mackey at the NCO club, we'd never have heard the whole story."

So that's where they went!

I considered saying that one of the junior leaders, Bill Compton, did know a good part of it, but I let it go.

"And finally," Captain Strom said, "Major Garrett suggested I review your case carefully. He said anybody in as much trouble as you were yesterday, who'd still notice a tree that needed protecting, belonged doing conservation work."

"All I did was fix a deer cage," I said.

"My view, too," the captain told me. "Count yourself lucky the major is a major and I'm a captain.

"In fact," he said, indicating it was time I left, "you ought to count yourself lucky all around."

Part II

Chapter 12

The first thing we did on the train was flip a seat-back so Nate and I could ride facing Sam and Apple. I said, "The captain told me you talked to Reese and Sergeant Mackey. Thank you."

Nate said, "It wasn't much."

"You'd have done the same for us," Sam said.

"If you ask me, it was too easy," Apple said. "I was all set to—"

"To what?" Nate asked.

"Well, I don't know," Apple said. "But I'd have thought of something, you can bet."

We had a good laugh, and then Sam turned to Nate. "So, we're going to your part of Montana. What's it like?"

"Farm and ranch country, mostly, or it was. The land's pretty shot." Nate shook his head. "I don't want to look a gift horse in the mouth, but I don't see what a CCC camp can do to change that."

Apple said, "What's confusing me is I thought the CCC was for forest work and parks."

"No," Sam said. "There are a lot of CCC camps under the Forest Service or National Park Service, but others do projects for state agencies, the Bureau of Reclamation, the Soil Conservation Service that the major said we'll be working for. I read about that before I signed on."

"You read up! Only you, Senator!" Apple said.

Sam took the ribbing good-natured.

Then we moved on to what we'd heard just before leaving Missoula: that Klein and Lukowski had been picked up not far out of town.

"What do you think's going to happen to them?" Apple asked.

"Something bad, I hope," Nate said. He'd lost six dollars to them and didn't have high hopes of getting it back. "I'm just glad we're done with them. Pair of bad apples, if you ask me."

"Hey! Watch how you talk about apples," Apple said.

Nate added, "I'm glad to be shut of Compton, too."

"No more than me," I said with feeling, and everybody laughed some more.

We were in high spirits, that was for sure.

It was almost night by the time we got to Monroe, where we were met by a driver and another stake truck outfitted with a canvas top and bench seats.

"Get your gear off the baggage car and pile in," Major Garrett ordered. "Unless I miss my guess, supper will be waiting for us."

The campsite was only a few miles away, but the roads were so bad, the trip took close to an hour. As we jolted along, I strained to see what I could. At first the rutted road ran straight, but then it angled off and became a double track that followed close to the edge of what Nate called a *coulee.*

It's what I knew as a gully—Texas was full of them—only this one was cut deeper than most I'd seen, threading between steep banks.

"Rain cut this?" I asked Nate.

"Rain combined with melted snow. Even dry as it is around here, springtime flooding can be a problem," he answered.

The truck made a sharp turn, plunged down one side of the coulee with a suddenness that made my stomach lurch, and then climbed up the far side, its wheels spinning in the dirt.

We came out on a field dotted with stacks of lumber and headed for a cluster of tents at the far side. Most were small, cone shaped, and dark, but lights glowed inside a large, rectangular one, and as soon as we pulled up before it, a man came out to greet us.

He was an old guy—well, maybe not old, but older than Major Garrett, anyway. Not a soldier. "About time!" he said, "I was just wondering if I'd have to eat the missus' chili all by my lonesome."

"Hello, Pops," the major greeted him. "What's this about Mrs. Jensen?"

"Oh, she brought over things so the young pups would find a good meal waiting. Got word the mess sergeant who's been assigned here won't get in until later. And I'm supposed to tell you he'll be bringing another couple of enrollees with him."

"I heard," the major said. "I brought along gear for them."

Over supper, we got to know Pops—Lester Jensen was his name, but he said we might as well call him Pops, since everybody else did. Once around the table, he'd learned all our names.

Supper was chili served in the mess kits we dug out of our barracks bags. I said, "This is about the best chili I ever ate, even in Texas."

Pops said, "The secret's in the meat. It's elk. Anytime you want more, you just go into town and look for the café. The missus runs it, and never a day goes by she don't make chili fresh."

"But you work here?" Sam asked him.

"I do," Pops answered. "I'm what's called a LEM. That's for local experienced man. The CCC's got me on the payroll same as you."

"Pops will be helping guide the construction work," Major Garrett said, "and after that he'll be staying on as a project foreman. You can thank him for having your tents set up."

"They're supposed to hold eight men, but that's crowding," Pops said. "I put up an extra so there's just five cots in each. You have the boys in squads?"

"No," the major answered. "They can sort themselves out."

Apple, Nate, Sam, and I moved into the first empty tent we came to. It *was* crowded, even with just the five beds that were arranged around a cranky-looking, cold stove.

"I don't know about you fellows," I said, "but I don't need a fire near as much I need some shut-eye. I'm turning in."

"Sounds good to me," Nate said, and in no time we had our flashlights turned off and were settled down. And in no time after that, it was morning again, and we were being waked up by a fellow we'd never met poking his head through the tent's flap.

"You guys got room for another?" he asked cheerfully.

Apple groaned and pulled his blankets over his head.

"We got a extra cot," I said. I sat up so I could see him better.

He looked young.

"Come on in," I said. "I'm Moss Trawnley, from Texas."

"Harold Sanders, Corvallis. On a farm near there, anyway. That's Montana."

"Nate Lundgren's a Montanan, too," I said, as Nate

waved a hand without getting up. "That mummy under the covers there is Apple Durgan from Tennessee, and—"

"Sam Whitney, Boston," Sam volunteered, making a face as his feet hit the cold floor. "Welcome."

Chapter 13

The new fellow didn't have much unpacking to do, not having been issued any gear yet, so he sat on his bed and visited while the rest of us got ourselves going.

"How come you got to skip conditioning camp?" Apple asked.

"I applied too late. But the selection agent I went to still hadn't filled his quota, so he was willing to look the other way on some things. He didn't even ask—"

He broke off, but I'd have laid good money he was going to say the agent hadn't even checked on Harold's age. If he was seventeen yet, I was a monkey's uncle.

If he was even *sixteen* yet, I was a monkey's uncle.

"Hey, Moss, that's my foot you're standing on!" Nate exclaimed.

"Sorry," I said. "This tent's going to take some getting used to."

"I've known chicken coops with more room," Apple said.

But Harold was surveying us happily. "Isn't this great?" he said. "Just like I hoped. Not the tents, I mean. I'd expected a regular camp, though I guess we're going to be building that, aren't we? But I mean, not a girl around..."

Apple looked at him disbelieving. "You don't like girls?"

"Well, I don't dislike them. But I joined up so I could stop living with them for a while. I got six sisters at home." Harold made a comical face. "And not another brother they can spread their bossing to.

"It's all the time, 'Harold, do this,' and 'Harold do that.' 'Harold, fix your collar, comb your hair, don't mumble.' 'Harold, I am going to wring your neck the next time you belch in front of a boyfriend I bring home.'"

His imitation of his sisters got us all laughing, though Apple said, "I wouldn't mind me a girl who was a little bossy, as long as she was pretty."

"Apple's in the market for a girlfriend," Nate explained.

By then we all pretty much knew each other's girlfriend status. Sam had broken off with his before he joined up, for just what reason I didn't know. Nate was between girls. I'd told them about Beatty, in a general way.

Harold said he hadn't thought much yet about girlfriends.

"How far's Corvallis?" Apple asked.

Harold looked alarmed. "Too far for my sisters to visit me here," he said. "Honest. I want to spend my six months without one time hearing someone say, 'Harold!'"

"That's going to be kind of hard," I said, "since that's your name."

"Unless you want a nickname," Sam said. "It seems to be a CCC tradition."

The four of us eyed the newcomer while we threw out suggestions that would fit. *Sandy. Short Stuff. Kid.*

"I got it," I said. "Romeo."

For a second there was silence, and then one by one the others started laughing.

"That's perfect," Apple said. "See, because Romeo was this romantic guy, and that's just what you're not, so..."

"Apple," Nate said. "We all got it."

Work began right after breakfast.

I'd expected to be pointed toward a pile of lumber and told which boards to carry where. Or maybe given a hammer and told what to start hammering on.

But instead, Pops unrolled a set of construction plans. The top one was a draftsman's drawing of what the finished camp would look like: a horseshoe of buildings around a central field. "Rec hall, machinery shop, garage, infirmary...," he said. "We're going to have us a regular town, but we'll have to get cracking to get it built before the rest of the company arrives."

The morning meeting was a regular thing, because Pops and the other LEMs were bound to see that us enrollees understood the why and how of each task we took on. First it was staking out the perimeters of buildings. Then it was preparing surfaces for the pillars that would support most of them and for the concrete slabs that would go under the shower house and garages.

"Getting the forms in for the concrete work is one job we want to get done before the ground freezes," Pops told us. "We can spread some tarps to keep warmth in, but we still ought to move fast."

Riley Maxwell, who was from Alabama, said, "You are joking, aren't you? Freeze like ice?"

"As hard as," Pops answered. "Hard enough you won't want to be pickaxing through it."

Not that that would have been much harder than a lot of the other stuff we did.

Once we were ready for the concrete work, we loaded cement, sand, gravel, and water—all in just the right proportions—into a big barrel that had a long-handled crank on one side. Then we took shifts, three of us at a time, leaning in with all our weight to keep the thing turning.

An East Coast city fellow named Con Hermiker looked truly perplexed. "How come we don't just get a mixing machine?" he asked.

"Because, son," Pops answered, "the CCC runs on muscle and elbow grease."

One of the farm boys added, "I never knew anything that didn't. Mainly mine, or some mule's."

It helped that what was strange to one fellow was familiar to another; it kept us, as a crew, from being all thumbs at any particular task. And in no time, we were pulling together to get the camp built on schedule.

Chapter 14

Once we got the concrete in, work really speeded up, mainly because of the clever way the CCC provided us with a lot of things already made, like the wall panels that arrived by truck. *Prefabricated,* they were called.

Pops said they came from a factory where they were being turned out by the hundreds, all the same and ready to put up.

We'd run floor joists and build the floor and sills. Then we'd raise a set of those prefabricated wall panels, join them together with ceiling rafters, and, *presto,* we'd have ourselves a shop, maybe, or an infirmary. Of course there'd still be the roof to put on, but that part went fast, being only boards covered with tar paper.

And there was finish work to do, of course. Lots of that.

An electrician from town gave us a quick course in stringing wire, which Nate proved especially good at.

"It's not all that different from stringing fence," he said, "except you don't want to stretch it."

It turned out that Apple had a knack for plumbing jobs, and Sam learned to fit joints prettier than anybody.

I sometimes needed to leave the construction detail long enough to work on a truck engine. Mostly, though, I was kind of an all-jobs builder, as was most of the fellows.

We slipped ball games in when we could, and loafed on Sunday afternoons, but the camp springing up around us was all the incentive we needed to keep our minds on our jobs. Day by day, we were getting better at them. Getting fond of showing how we could do a thing, too.

Which maybe was why it was easy to get grouchy when things didn't go right and all we had to show was wounded pride and a mistake.

Romeo was the worst for making mistakes though he tried the hardest of anybody. He just couldn't pound a nail without bending it crooked or drill a hole without breaking a drill bit. And somehow he latched onto me as his favorite person to work with. "Your shadow," Nate joked.

I shrugged. "I don't mind," I said. "He reminds me of my brothers."

Though I did lose my temper with Romeo when he made me look bad before Pops.

I'd been preparing to cut some shelf boards to go inside a cabinet when Romeo volunteered to help. "I can cut them while you put up the supports," he said.

I had misgivings, but he looked so eager, I agreed. "They need to be twenty-nine inches each," I told him. I wrote it on a slip of paper so he couldn't forget. "Four of them, each twenty-nine inches," I repeated. "And remember, measure twice, cut once."

"I'll measure three times," Romeo promised.

I was still nailing in the two-by-two supports when he brought over a stack of neatly cut boards. "Done in time for lunch," he said. "Want me to do anything else before I knock off?"

"Nah, I got this," I said. "I'll catch up with you in the mess tent."

I was so close to finishing the supports that I pushed on. And then, just to see how the whole thing was going to look, I tried setting one of the shelves inside.

Pops came over just as I angled it into position, only to have it fall right through the supports and clatter onto the floor.

My first thought was I'd somehow set it in wrong. But of course I hadn't. The board was too short.

"What'd you do, try to eyeball it?" Pops asked me. "Or make your measurements without checking the blueprints first? Learning to follow blueprints is part of your job."

His criticism was mild enough, but I felt my face flaming. I hadn't read the prints—like most of the fellows, I'd avoided figuring out how—but that wasn't the point.

"I measured inside the cabinet, instead," I said. "Look!" I grabbed a tape measure and showed him. "Twenty-nine inches, just like I told Romeo." I picked up the shelf and laid the measure on that. Twenty-seven inches.

"That—" I held back the name I was about to call my friend, but I thought it.

"Romeo," I said, catching him halfway through the meal. "I told you to make those boards twenty-nine inches."

"I did," he said. "Two feet, three inches."

Sam opened his mouth and then clamped it shut without saying a word.

"Why?" Romeo asked.

"Because you cut them short," I said. "Two feet, three inches...can't you add? That's twenty-seven, not twenty-nine. How could you make a mistake like that?"

"I thought..."

"You didn't even have to add. Just read the numbers on the tape measure."

"You were using it. I used a ruler."

"A foot ruler? Of all the numskull..."

"Hey, Moss," Apple said, "it was just a few boards."

The distress on his face—and the misery on Romeo's—caught me up short. What had got into me?

"I'm really sorry, Moss," Romeo said.

"Forget it," I told him. "It was just a few boards. I should have done them myself."

Then it was Nate looking undecided about saying something that he ended up keeping to himself.

And Pops, eating down at the end of the table, didn't say anything, either.

I thought on it while I was cutting new boards and kept thinking the rest of the day. Truth to tell, I didn't know why I'd jumped on Romeo the way I had. Those boards *weren't* a big thing.

I guessed maybe I'd just been mad at myself for depending on him to start with. It was like my pa had always said: If you want a job done right, do it yourself.

That was back before he stopped doing any job at all, of course.

The thing was, every time I looked across the room and saw Romeo, his good nature knocked to pieces, I felt like I was the one who'd been doing the letting down.

Finally, late in the day, I asked him to help me place some cabinet hinges.

"Aw, you better get somebody else," he said. "Hinges are tricky."

"I know," I said. "That's why the job's going to take four hands."

"You got it marked where they'll go?"

"Yeah. But you can check me."

———————

Later on, after work, Pops caught up with me. "Glad you fixed that mistake," he said.

"Cutting the extra boards wasn't anything," I said. "Sorry about the wasted wood, though."

"We'll find a use for it. But those short boards weren't the mistake I was talking about."

I said, "Oh."

Chapter 15

Even if I was in the clear with Pops again, his criticism from the day before still stung.

So at break time later that morning, when a snow squall had everyone drinking their coffee under the canvas shelter where the work plans were laid out, I declined to join a card game.

Instead I went over to the blueprints, which were stretched out on a plank laid across sawhorses. I moved one of the rocks that were anchoring them down, so I could read the legend under it. SHOWER HOUSE.

I studied the ruler-straight white lines, some dashed and some solid, and the neat, slanted numerals that were everywhere. I didn't see how anybody made sense of them.

Though of course that was what Beatty thought about the radio schematics I followed, back at the airport in Texas. "It's a mystery to me," she once said, "how you can turn a diagram that's all lines and notations into the insides of a radio."

I'd told her, "It's no harder than those airplane maintenance manuals you're always poring over."

A burst of talk interrupted my recollections. Nate was looking openmouthed surprised while the others were glad-handing Apple over a pinochle trick he'd just swiped from under Nate's nose.

I guess you can learn anything if you want to bad enough, I thought.

I identified a few offset lines as doors and windows and was puzzling over some symbols when Pops came in to call everyone back to work.

He looked over my shoulder at the symbol near where my finger was resting. "Electrical outlet," he said. "And that one there"—he pointed to a line that alternated long dashes with short ones—"that's for a hot water line."

At break time that afternoon, and at the next and the next, I returned to the blueprints, and gradually they became less mysterious. I knew I was getting them right when Pops had the guys cut a stack of twelve two-by-twelves down to boards eleven feet seven inches long.

Floor joists, I said to myself, picturing where I'd seen that eleven feet seven inches on the blueprints. Sure enough, once the lumber was cut, Pops said, "Okay, let's go make us a floor."

It made me feel downright competent.

And almost as pleased with myself as when I came up with an idea for Romeo.

———

Fall was on the run by now, and in the mornings we needed a fire in the wood-burning Sibley stove in our tent.

It was such a stubborn, ill-tempered contraption we gave it a name—Bad Beulah—and daily wasted time groaning and arguing about whose turn it was to get out of bed first and feed fuel into her.

One especially chilly morning we put off even the arguing with a discussion about all the things we wished the mess sergeant would make for breakfast. His standbys were pancakes and oatmeal, which we'd been eating, one on one day and the other on the next, without letup.

"I could eat scrambled eggs with bacon done crisp but the fat still chewy," Apple said. "And hush puppies."

"Brook trout, pan fried," Nate suggested.

"I'd go for a cinnamon sweet roll," Romeo said. "Hot, with the icing still melting. Almost big across as a dinner plate, that's how I like to make 'em."

"*You* make them?" Nate said, sounding disbelieving. "You know how to bake?"

"You keep forgetting those six sisters I got. When I was growing up, whichever one was minding me made me pitch into whatever other job she had," Romeo said. "Besides," he added, "they're all always watching their figures. If I'd left dessert making to them, I wouldn't have gotten anything but Jell-O. They like that for making their fingernails strong."

"So you came here to get it, instead," Sam said.

Jell-O was another of the mess sergeant's standbys. Green on Sundays, Tuesdays, and Thursdays. Red the other days.

I thought about Romeo's baking skills while I ate breakfast—it was an oatmeal morning—and I decided to trust Romeo hadn't just been talking. Afterward I lingered to have a word with Major Garrett, hoping he wouldn't mind me putting my oar in where it hadn't been asked.

"Sir," I said, "I've got this idea. There's a guy in our tent—Harold Sanders—who's a real talented cook. And if you don't mind my saying so, our meals—not that I'm not grateful for them, but a body can eat just so much oatmeal—and..."

I kind of thought the major was struggling to hold back a laugh, and I thought maybe I really had spoken out of turn.

Regardless, soon after, Romeo got temporarily detailed to help the mess sergeant. And that first morning, when he set a tray of cinnamon rolls on the table, smelling of yeast and swimming in butter, you'd have thought from the cheers that rang out, we'd all found a pot of gold.

Major Garrett, admiring a forkful just dripping with icing, reassigned Romeo to the kitchen permanent, on the spot.

Chapter 16

Things turned difficult right after that, when the winter Pops had warned about moved in.

One evening I had the passing notion the air had a sharper bite to it than usual.

"Smells like snow," Nate said, but I thought he was putting me on, despite the flurries we'd seen. People didn't smell snow.

The next morning, we woke to a temperature of ten degrees and a blanket of white. The powdery snow wasn't deep, but it blew into our faces and down our necks.

From then on, nobody bathed till it was absolutely necessary, since our temporary shower was a canvas-sided closet beneath a fifty-five-gallon drum. Icy water poured out of holes poked in the drum's bottom, while a hose connected to a pump at the camp well kept the drum filled. What showers did get taken tended to be brief.

Just like visits to the latrine.

The camp didn't have a working inside toilet yet, though the cold sure made getting one built a priority. Meanwhile, we had to suffer with more canvas hung around a board seat over a pit. And hung on just three sides, too. The fourth side, which was left open to a view of the prairie, let in as much wind as scenery.

It made for humor, and we needed it, being discouraged by how our camp-building progress had slowed way, way down. The delay was partly due to some roofing materials not showing up when they should have, but mostly it was due to the cold making any chore take twice as long.

Gloves made nails hard to pick up. Tar had to be heated forever before it could be spread. Glass seemed to crack extra easy, making setting in windowpanes a special difficulty.

None of us realized how proud we'd been of all we'd accomplished, until the forced slowdown made it suddenly doubtful we'd get the camp done on time. After all, to be able to say we'd built a camp—*a whole camp*—in under six weeks! *That* would be something to write home about.

Without anybody asking us to, we upped our work hours till by the short days of mid-December we were going from can't see to can't see, and on either side of that, too. The morning work would begin under big lights that ran off electric cables we'd strung into camp from the county power lines. Sometimes we'd put in a couple of hours before breakfast.

And we finished up under electric lights, too.

We tried to keep each other hopeful. If you asked any fellow how a job was going, he'd say, "Almost there!"

But at lunchtime on the Friday before the main company was to arrive, Major Garrett asked for our attention. We were eating in the mess hall, which was the only building 100 percent done.

He said, "It's time we did a reassessment. Nobody could have worked harder than you boys have, and you have every right to be proud of what you've accomplished. But we're going to have to accept that the camp's not going to be ready to move into by Monday. Close, but there are just too many things undone, in the barracks in particular."

Murmurs of disappointment floated about. "But where will everybody stay?" someone asked.

"I've requested troop tents from district headquarters," the major answered. "It won't hurt the new guys to sleep under canvas a few nights. Make them appreciate what you've done. And now I want you to knock off early today and go enjoy yourselves with an evening in town."

"We'd as soon keep on working," Sam said, looking around to the rest of us for agreement. We all nodded.

"A few hours isn't going to make the difference between our finishing things before Monday and not," the major told him. "I'd like to give you the whole weekend off, but once the tents arrive I'm going to need you to start putting them up."

Pops went with us into Monroe, where he gave us some last-minute instructions. "You're on your own," he said, "but I'll expect you to meet up back here by eight thirty. You'll find the café open—the missus will probably give you a good price on supper if you want to go in there. There's the pool hall. Movie theater—"

He was interrupted by a car that passed us, stopped, and then backed up. Mr. Schieling, the selection agent who'd enrolled me in the CCC, got out.

"Pops Jensen!" he said. "I've been wondering when your boys were going to get some time off!" He turned to us. "Life all right at that camp? I've got some spare change I've been wondering how to spend. Can I treat you to ice cream? Or hot cocoa?"

Some of the guys were already peeling off, mostly heading toward the pool hall. Sam left to investigate Monroe's library. Others, though, including Apple and Romeo, nodded a yes.

Nate said to me, "I think I'll hike on out to see my folks. Want to come along?"

"I'd like to," I answered. "If you don't think I'll be in the way."

Before we started off, we thanked Mr. Schieling for his offer.

He studied me a moment. "Oh yes," he said. "Moss Trawnley. How do you like the CCC?"

"It's great," I said. "I really do thank you for getting me in."

He waved off my appreciation. "You made that decision yourself," he said. "All you boys did. And now you and Nate remember, you have a rain check for that ice cream or cocoa, since I can't talk you into any today."

As we headed out of town, I thought about how I'd answered Mr. Schieling. The CCC *was* great, and it scared me to think how close I'd come to miss being a part of it. I still got mad every time I remembered how Pa had more or less forced me to strike out on my own, but, of course, if he hadn't...

But what if that justice of the peace hadn't given me the newspaper story about enrollment being open? Or if I'd gotten off the train at some town where the selection agent had already filled his quota? Or if my friends hadn't helped keep me from getting thrown out of conditioning camp, after that fight I got in?

I glanced over at Nate, whose idea of walking home was to get out of Pops's sight and then stick out his thumb. Hitchhiking was against CCC rules, but Nate's view was that catching a ride in your hometown didn't count.

He was saying, "I don't know why Maggie doesn't

like Owen Schieling. He knocks himself out being nice."

"Yes, he does," I agreed.

I'd almost forgotten Nate had a sister, but now I asked, "You think Maggie will be home?"

"I don't know why not, once school's out," he answered. "She doesn't have anyplace else to go. Hey! There's somebody slowing for us now."

Chapter 17

Nate lived along a washboard road where working farms alternated with abandoned ones. He pointed out the start of his place, with its bare fields neatly plowed into straight furrows. The recent snow had melted, leaving long ridges of wet earth.

A dirt driveway between outbuildings led to the Lundgren house, a two-story farmhouse in bad need of paint. We found Mrs. Lundgren in the kitchen, which smelled of something spicy being baked.

"Hope there's plenty," Nate said, giving her a hug. "This is my friend Moss Trawnley. I've been bragging on your cooking, so he's come with an appetite."

"Supper's hours off," she said, "but I've got cookies about to come out of the oven." She stood back to get a good look at him. "Oh, I've missed you."

"Who's here?" a hoarse voice asked, as Maggie came into the kitchen wrapped in a heavy robe. Her nose was red, her eyes were watery, and she took one look at me and whirled on her brother. "Nate, you should have warned us..."

"It's just Moss," he said. "He doesn't care how you look."

Before disappearing back up the stairs, she gave him a glare that made him say, "What? What!"

Then Nate's dad came in the back door.

"Arne," Mrs. Lundgren said to him, "Nate's here with one of his friends. This is Moss Trawnley."

"Glad to meet you, Moss," Mr. Lundgren said. "Welcome home, son."

Mr. Lundgren was built stocky, like Nate, with thinning hair and faded eyes. He went over to the sink, pumped a panful of water, and scrubbed his hands before sitting down at the table.

Mrs. Lundgren poured coffee around and then moved the cookies—Russian rocks, she called them—straight from the oven to a cooling rack she set before us. "Moss," she said. "Tell me how they are."

It was a good thing she had a second tray baking, because we polished that first batch off in no time, and managed to get in a good bit of talking, too.

Nate started to tell about camp, but his mother stopped that. "Might as well wait on your sister," she said, "or you're going to have to say it all over."

Mr. Lundgren asked, "What's your father do, Moss?"

I glanced at Nate, who was watching to see what I'd answer. The guys hadn't pried, since I'd let it be known my business was my business, but he was curious.

I said, "He used to be a farmer, before going into some other things. Mechanics, mainly."

"Wish I knew more about machines," Mr. Lundgren said. "I've got a tractor that gives me more problems than horses ever did." He shot a look at Nate. "I shouldn't have listened to people urging me to make the change."

All around, it was an uncomfortable few moments for Nate and me both. I tried to help by asking, "Are you having a problem with the tractor now?"

"The thing's gone underpowered on me. It was working good enough up until a month or so ago, but now I can't get it to pull what it should."

"How's the engine sound?" I asked.

"Rough."

"The ignition timing out of adjustment?"

"Could be. I don't have a way to test for it."

"Maybe run it up a hill?"

He looked puzzled.

"Something my pa taught me, 'cause we didn't have a timing light, either. If you'd like, I'll show you."

I loosened the distributor cap and turned it so the spark plugs would fire just a tad earlier. "When there's a load on," I said, "you want sparks to hit the gasoline that's squirting in just a instant before the pistons hit the top of their cycle. It gives the explosion a chance to build force."

I tightened back up on the distributor. "Can we try it?"

Mr. Lundgren ran the tractor up a steep bank, which was a quick way to see how it would handle a call for power. "Better," he said, coming back. "But not quite right."

So we advanced the spark some more, and some more again, running the tractor up the bank each time, till we advanced the spark too far. And then we backed it to the perfect spot, so the engine was working just right.

"That was one slick trick Moss taught me," Mr. Lundgren told his family. "I learned something."

We were gathered around the table again, this time for pot roast and mashed potatoes, gravy, and string beans. Maggie was with us now, in a dress. She smelled of cough syrup, and she'd put on some powdery stuff to tone down the color of her nose.

"Did Dad show you around?" she asked me.

"Some. You've got a nice place."

"Glad you can see that," Mr. Lundgren said. "Some people don't seem able to."

"Dad," Nate said, "you know—"

"Please," Mrs. Lundgren broke in. "Don't you two start."

Searching for something peaceable to say, I asked Mr. Lundgren, "How long have you been here?"

"Since 1912," he answered. "There wasn't a thing here when Mrs. Lundgren and I staked out our section corners."

"Just open land?"

"Prairie and breaks. Our first year here we cut sod for the front wall of a house we built into a hill. It's Mrs. Lundgren's cold cellar now. We put our first crop into the raw ground we'd exposed."

"What did you plant?"

"Just garden produce that year, so we wouldn't starve. But by the next spring we'd broken enough land to put in a wheat crop." Mr. Lundgren's eyes looked someplace past me. "This is wheat country. You wait and see, young man. We're due for a crop that'll be something to talk about."

Nate and Maggie exchanged glances, and Mrs. Lundgren pressed her lips together.

"Dad," Nate said, "you know the chances of that are—"

"I told you, not now, Nate!" Mrs. Lundgren said. "Maggie, maybe this is the time to ask those questions you had about the CCC."

"I've been storing them up!" Maggie declared. "Moss, Nate has not written one letter home. I bet you're writing back to Texas, aren't you?"

"Well, I..."

"I want to know all about the camp and who the other fellows are. What the soldiers are like. Is it true that one of the camp's projects is going to be planting trees? Because—"

"Whoa!" Mr. Lundgren said. "Moss, don't mind my daughter. Sometimes she seems more like a rolling locomotive than a well-mannered female."

"I won't," I said and then realized my answer made it sound like I agreed with the description. "I'm used to it," I elaborated. "I've got three sisters."

The silence that followed told me I hadn't fixed much, so I plunged into answering the only one of Maggie's questions I could remember.

"I don't know about the tree planting," I said. "We've been so busy trying to get the camp built, nobody's been talking about what we're going to do once it's done."

"Folks are discussing it around here," Maggie said. "In a town small as ours, talking's the main entertainment, and people do a lot of it at the mercantile."

She told her father, "My boss says he heard the government wants to plant trees and shrubs, a lot of them, along stream banks and gullies. If the government wants to put some on private land, we ought to volunteer ours."

"I don't have any land to give to the government," Mr. Lundgren said.

"I didn't mean for us to give away anything," Maggie said. "But if the government's looking for places—"

Nate broke in. "What she means is if the government's after eroded land to fix up, we've sure got it."

Mr. Lundgren's neck darkened. "Ours isn't worse

than elsewhere," he said. "And when we get some
rain—"

"Dad, you say the same thing year after year: that
we need rain. We're in a drought, and our land's so
messed up the rain we do get causes as much harm as
good. Between drought and outdated practices—"

"Nate!" Mrs. Lundgren's voice was sharp. "That's
enough!"

Mr. Lundgren looked hard at his son. "When this
place is yours, you can experiment all you want.
Meanwhile, my job's seeing that it produces enough to
keep this family afloat.

"And if *you* want to do something meanwhile, you
might try letting Moss teach you a thing or two. He
seems to have his head on his shoulders a lot more
solid than you ever have."

Chapter 18

As soon as we were outside, I told Nate, "I'm sorry about that. I didn't mean to get between you and your pa."

"I'm just sorry you got dragged into one of our arguments." Nate slammed his hand against a post. "He is the most bullheaded man!"

"Wait up, you two," Maggie called, pulling on her coat as she ran down from the house. "Mom says you can take the truck in. I'll drive it back."

Nate slid behind the steering wheel, and I followed Maggie in the other side. She said, "I didn't think Mom would let me go since I didn't go to school, but then she said okay. I wasn't all that sick anyway."

"You stay home to help Dad finish up that fence section he was working on?" Nate asked.

"We'd be crazy not to get it done before snow piles up. So, Nate, why were you beating on that post just now? Are you still upset from supper?"

"I was telling Moss I wish Dad weren't so afraid to try something new."

"The trees?" Maggie said. "That's just rumor."

"To try *anything*. Maybe even moving off our place and going where he wouldn't always have two strikes against him."

"Nate! You don't mean that! This is our home. I love it more than I could ever love anyplace else in the whole world."

Nate's voice softened. "I know you do, sis. But we've gone round about this before. I don't want a lifetime of worries from trying to make this land be something it's not."

"The last I heard, you weren't planning one," she said stiffly. "You were planning a college career, so you could study farming instead of doing it."

"The last I heard," he told her, "planning and doing were two different things."

They sounded more angry *for* than *at* each other.

Then Nate said, "Moss, if you get the chance, you ought to read how this part of the country once was. And not that long ago. Short-grass prairie stretching hundreds of miles, feeding herds of bison and antelope, and then open-range cattle after that. Homesteaders went elsewhere, where farming made sense.

"But then the good land got scarce. You ever hear of Hardy Webster Campbell?" Nate said the name like it was poison.

"No."

"He was big on dryland farming, telling people they could turn semiarid plains into cropland. That it was all right to plow up the sod. Campbell said it didn't matter that the land got hardly any rain, because the trick lay in how you worked the surface. Lots of tilling."

Nate waved a hand toward the dark fields outside the car. "It meant lots of topsoil left naked: unprotected, unanchored. Putting stock into such theories made about as much sense as believing that rain follows the plow, but there're people still willing to believe that. My dad and the others scrambling to hang on around here—they're all next-year farmers."

"Next-year farmers?" I asked.

"Fools who always think their luck's going to turn the next year."

"Nate," Maggie said, "you shouldn't talk that way."

"I'll talk how I want and think how I want, too."

I felt for Nate, but I also felt for Mr. Lundgren. He put me in the mind of my own pa, before just too many things turned wrong despite a lifetime of doing his best. Only Mr. Lundgren wasn't giving up, and he wasn't walking out on anybody.

I said, "It must be hard to hear that what you've spent years doing has been wrong. You'd feel betrayed, like whatever you put your faith in let you down. And you'd think twice before giving your trust again."

Maggie's head turned sharply toward mine. "That's what Nate doesn't understand," she said.

We drove three, maybe five minutes before Nate quietly said, "Yes, I do."

We said our good-byes to Maggie and leaned against the camp truck to wait for the other fellows.

"Look," I told Nate, "Major Garrett said the reason we're out here is to help the Monroe area. Maybe we will."

"Sure," Nate said. "When we couldn't even put a few buildings up the way we'd planned."

"They're almost done."

"Not on schedule."

A commotion moved down the street. "Sounds like our crew," I said.

It was, and the commotion was over a box of pies Pops was carrying. "Don't know why the missus spoils you boys." He settled the box on the truck's front seat, telling Dave Malcomb, the CCC'er who was driving, "Now don't you sample more than one." Then Pops climbed in the back with everybody else.

"You going back to camp for the night?" someone asked him.

"Yeah, I want to get an early start on the work tomorrow. So, did everybody hit all Monroe's hot spots?"

"Such as they were," Riley Maxwell said. "Or we tried to."

"We got thrown out of the bar," Hal Linchfeld volunteered.

"Never let in, you mean!" someone said.

"And the movie was *A Farewell to Arms,* from three years ago," complained a Los Angeles fellow who went by Cal.

Riley gibed him, "That didn't keep you from going in, or from coming out with three girls you went and bought sodas for. You got any money left?"

"Not much," Cal answered. "But it was money well spent. Kind of an investment in the future, so I'll have a partner at that dance the major's been promising."

Pops told him, "Treating one girl to a soda's an investment. But three—seems to me, that's courting trouble."

"Where did you disappear to, Moss?" Riley asked. "You go off with a girl?"

Nate answered, "He came home with me."

Talk halted while the truck negotiated an especially bad stretch of road. Then Apple suddenly said, "We came pretty close, didn't we?"

"You mean to doing all Monroe's attractions?" Hal asked.

"No, he means to getting our camp finished. Don't you, Apple?" Sam said.

"Yeah. I keep thinking what a shame it is we won't quite make it. Almost worse than if we'd got nowhere near."

"That's true," Riley said. "I was thinking it before."

"Just remember what the major told you," Pops said. "What with all that has been accomplished, you've done yourselves proud."

I woke up knowing I hadn't been asleep long. It was eleven, maybe? The fire, visible through the grill in the stove door, made the tent roof look red.

The breathing sounds were off a bit; too few of them, I realized. Someone was missing. I rolled over and looked around. Romeo's cot was empty.

I laid there for a while, expecting him to return from a quick trip to the bushes. But eventually, when he didn't, I got up, pulled on some clothes and fumbled with my boots.

"What are you doing?" Sam whispered.

"Going to see what Romeo's up to."

"I'll go with you."

"No need," I said, but Sam was already reaching for his own things.

Chapter 19

We checked the latrine to start with, shining our flash-lights inside as the tail of some animal slipped away under one cloth wall. Sam said, "Remind me not to use this place without looking first. Where next?"

"The mess hall maybe?"

But before we got there, we spotted a light on in the shower house. Along with the barracks, it was one of the buildings we'd really hoped to have completed before Monday.

And sure enough, Romeo was inside, a piece of pipe in each hand and some pipe fittings on the floor in front of him, a totally perplexed expression on his face.

"What are you doing?" Sam asked from the doorway.

Romeo jumped about a mile, and then looked from one to the other of us sheepishly. "Everybody's so let down over the camp not getting done like we'd hoped, and here I've been messing in the kitchen instead of helping build. So I was just going to see if I couldn't figure out something I could do to move things along."

I was at a loss for words, and for once, Sam seemed to be, too. Briefly. Then he said, "That's a good thought, Romeo, but maybe it's one best acted on tomorrow morning."

"You think?" Romeo asked.

"Yes, I do," Sam answered.

We'd almost gotten back to our tent when I halted. "You two go on," I told them.

"Where are you going?" Romeo asked.

"Over to the barracks."

"I'll roust the others," he said happily. "Just our tent, I mean."

"Nate and Apple aren't going to like it," I said. "Apple especially."

They came over, Apple still rubbing his eyes when he got a hammer and headed for the coatrack he'd been working on earlier. "I must be crazy to let myself get talked out of a good night's sleep," he told me.

"I didn't talk you out of anything," I said.

"And likely as not, whatever I do is going to need redoing, because I'm not downright sure I understand just how this is supposed to go."

"The blueprints ought to show it," I said.

"Yeah, if you can read blueprints."

I went over to the makeshift table where plans were laid out, and shuffled through them till I came to one that showed the details of the rack. "This doesn't look too hard. If you just take that long piece..."

The door opened, and Riley Maxwell and Hal Linchfeld came in. "Someone having a party?" Riley asked.

"You want to give me a job?" Hal said.

"Get in line behind me," Apple told him. "Moss can only boss one person at a time."

I was showing Hal where a window frame needed finishing when his and Riley's tent mates arrived, and then, by ones and twos, the fellows from the remaining tents showed up. Pretty soon everybody but me was working hard—even Romeo, who was sanding down a railing. But every time I picked up a hammer or screwdriver, I got stopped by someone asking, "Trawnley, what should I do next?"

"Look!" I finally told them all. "I'm not the boss of this job."

"Someone's got to be," Riley said. "And it wasn't my idea to come back to work."

"I didn't—"

"Trawnley!" he said. "Just tell us what to do and let us do it, and then we can all go to bed!" But he said it joking-like, and I realized that none of the guys actually expected to get any sleep.

I couldn't think what to answer, so I studied the blueprints some more. "Okay, then," I said. "Sam and Nate, why don't you..."

Along about 0100 or so, everybody was working so well that I even got to turn my hand to installing a rack that needed putting up. And then, without warning, Major Garrett and Pops showed up at the door, hard-to-read expressions on their faces.

As one after another of the guys spotted them, hammering and sawing left off till the room was dead quiet.

"We didn't think we'd wake you, Major," I ventured. "You either, Pops. We tried to keep it down."

The major started to say something and then stopped, and then Pops began to say something and then held it back, also.

And then the next thing, the two of them were taking off their coats and the major was saying, "It looks like you boys might need some help. You want to give us our orders?"

Everybody looked at me. And then, because I was about to lose my grip on the rack I'd been struggling to screw in place, I said, "Maybe if one of you wouldn't mind holding this?"

And then I added, "And Nate could use a hand running that cable."

They pitched in like I'd suggested, and when Pops finished helping Nate, he didn't head for the blueprints but instead waited for me to give him a new task. And the major rolled up his sleeves higher and waited, too, for me to tell him what to do next.

Romeo left long enough to make a big pot of coffee, which he brought over along with biscuits and sliced ham.

Riley lugged over a radio, and plugged it in.

"You're not going to find anything this time of night," Nate said.

But Riley fiddled with the tuner until he picked up a station playing dance music. *Must be good cloud cover,* I thought, *bouncing signals.* I leaned back for a moment, enjoying it and thinking what a satisfying night this was.

And then Nate called, "Hey, Trawnley, just 'cause you're bossing this job doesn't give you leave to stop working!"

We didn't knock off until dawn, when the mess sergeant came in to say he'd got both pancakes *and* oatmeal ready. By then a couple of partitions were the biggest things left to put up in one of the barracks, and electricity was the only major thing still needed in the other. But there were still lots and lots of smaller jobs undone.

Pops and the major had their heads together over breakfast, and I guessed they were trying to decide whether to go for a big final push or to play it safe and have us start setting up troop tents.

The tents were outside now, ready to be unloaded from a couple of army trucks that had shown up at daybreak. Another truck had brought in Sibley stoves, all of them needing to be set up.

Finally the major stood and looked over at us. "I know what you boys would like to do," he said. "But Pops and I haven't come to a conclusion yet. There are a number of things to consider. Meanwhile, I want everyone to hit the sack for a couple of hours of sleep. No arguing."

When we reassembled, yawning but hopeful, we found Pops posting a three-page list of chores that still needed doing, mostly in the barracks and the shower house. The list went from putting lightbulbs in all the ceiling fixtures to setting up eighty double bunks. "Pick a job," he said. "Do it. Check it off. Pick another."

Someone asked, "Do you and the major think we really can finish?"

Pops answered, "He's in writing a memo to the army, explaining why we won't be needing those squad tents after all."

Saw blades and drill bits got hot with use as we made our final push through the weekend. Mostly we stopped just long enough to gobble down some grub. Sometimes someone would stretch out on the floor, pillow his head on a jacket, and catch a few minutes of shut-eye, but nobody asked to quit. Finally, on Sunday evening, we reached the last item on Pops's list, which was to do a final sweepup in all the buildings.

I carried a carton of wood scraps to the trash bin for burning the next morning, and on my way back, I admired the sight of lighted windows in building after building. Figures moved back and forth under bulbs that hung from rafters.

I counted the structures: infirmary, down on one end of the central field; the shop; the garage...four, five, six...and on the opposite side, the mess hall and the two long barracks buildings and headquarters office, the rec hall...twelve.

We'd done all that. All that!

I saw other guys carrying out loads of trash, and every one of them stopped and looked.

Supper, which we didn't get to till going on 2030 hours, was stew, and as far as I could tell, it was none the worse for being cooked an extra couple of hours.

We took our time eating, and even after the coffeepot was empty, still nobody got up. Gradually the chatter died away, though, and everyone looked to the major.

He cleared his throat before saying, "I told you the other night that you should be proud of what you've done here. That was true then, but it's even more true now. You came up against what seemed like an impossible challenge, and you met it. Maybe in the long run, knowing you did that is what will count the most."

Apple said what I was feeling, and what the others probably were, too. "I'm kind of sorry we're done," he said. "I mean, that we're through being together as a construction team. I want..." He stopped as a knot traveled up his throat and back down.

Then Nate said, "Apple, your problem is that once the whole company arrives, there'll be too many guys for Pops's wife to bake pies for."

"That's it," Apple said, "what I was going to say."

Chapter 20

As guys began leaving the mess hall, Major Garrett said, "Moss, Sam, you two got a moment?"

I turned back, puzzled, but along with Sam answered, "Sure."

The major motioned for us to sit down again. Then, elbows on the table, he said, "I apologize for holding you up, but tomorrow's likely to be so busy, we won't get a chance to talk.

"As you know, the CCC has several goals—top among them to provide jobs and training while accomplishing important conservation work."

Sam and I exchanged glances. Why were we hearing this again, now?

"It's an ambitious program," the major went on, "and it works partly because CCC'ers themselves help run it. There are provisions for promoting the best of the enrollees to administrative and leadership positions, and with the main company arriving, I've got a couple of slots I need to fill."

He turned to Sam. "One of them is running the canteen, and I'd like you to take over that."

"The store, you mean?" Sam asked, referring to a counter and small stockroom we'd built at one end of the rec hall.

"That's right. It'll need to be open from seven to nine every evening," the major answered. "But the job's more than selling candy bars and soda pops. You'll have to track inventory, do the ordering, keep the accounts. Not by yourself, of course. You'll get guidance from my staff, which will be enlarged come tomorrow. And you'll be assigned another enrollee who'll help you at the store window and take over on your nights off."

I nodded, figuring that's where I would come in.

But then the major turned to me. "And, Moss, I'd like you to take a junior leader slot. You're young for the job, both agewise and in CCC experience, but I believe you're up to it."

I was so surprised I hardly knew what to say. I stammered something like a thank-you. "But I'm not... I've never...What would I have to do?"

"Your responsibilities would vary," the major said. "But, basically, you'd be the junior leader for one of the barracks. You'd have military staff over you, of course, but you'd sit in on administrative meetings, help the staff see that things get done, take care of your guys and represent them, and represent the camp's management, too."

I swallowed hard. What Major Garrett was describing…maybe Sam could do all that. "Sir," I said, "I don't think…"

The major went on like I hadn't interrupted. "I almost forgot to mention that a pay change comes with the promotions. Both jobs earn an extra fifteen dollars a month, so you'd each go from thirty to forty-five dollars. You can give me your answers in the morning."

After a bit more talk, Sam and I left, but a few steps out, I stopped.

Going back inside, I said to the major, "Why me, sir? If you don't mind me asking?"

"Why do you think?"

I hadn't expected him to turn the question back on me. "I suppose," I said, "because of the barracks work the other night? I didn't mean to take over. The bossing just kind of slipped out."

He chuckled. "I will say it's been a long while since anybody less than a colonel has ordered me about." He shot me a look. "And I don't expect that you ever will again."

"No, sir."

"But whether 'bossing'—as you put it—was your intention or not, the other boys did look to you for direction. That's important.

"But I based my decision more on other qualities. How you take criticism, for instance. When Pops jumped on you for not reading blueprints, you took it on yourself to figure out how.

"And you take responsibility for your work. I know that you had to learn that."

Romeo and those boards, I thought.

"And lastly, you figured out what to do with Romeo—Enrollee Sanders. He's a fine asset to the camp, but if you hadn't seen where he'd best fit in, he might have become the camp's first failure." The major laughed. "And we might never have gotten a breakfast that wasn't pancakes or oatmeal."

"Romeo's the one who knows how to bake," I said.

"Only he didn't think to volunteer that information to anyone. You did."

"I still don't see—"

"Moss," the major said, "the CCC isn't the army, and arguing with the camp's commanding officer doesn't go against any regulations. But I most strongly suggest you stop arguing and put this on."

He pulled a felt armband from his pocket and laid it on the table. It was green, with white letters that said LEADER.

My hand moved toward it and then pulled back.

"Can I still think on it overnight, sir?" I asked.

His face worked, and then he threw back his head and laughed harder than he had yet. "Yes, Enrollee Moss Trawnley, you can think on it overnight!"

His voice followed me out the door. "But then take it!"

Think on it! What I wanted to do was go to sleep and forget the whole scary idea.

Fifteen dollars a month extra to send home to my family—Ma could use it so many ways. Buy food, take the kids to a doctor when they needed it, maybe buy material for new dresses for my sisters. I doubted the youngest had ever had one that wasn't a hand-me-down.

Looked at that way, I didn't see how I could refuse the promotion.

But there was so much about the idea I didn't like. I'd made some friends, and I worried getting promoted over them might change things.

Or maybe it was just being promoted over them that I didn't like. The major had said I'd need to represent the other fellows, take care of them.

Maybe I *couldn't.* Minding my own self was hard enough.

And if I took on the job and failed at it, everybody would know.

I punched down my pillow for the umpteenth time and heard Sam say, his voice low, "You aiming to kill that thing?"

"Maybe."

"For what it's worth," he said, "I think the major's made a good choice."

I was heading to breakfast the next morning when Apple caught up with me. "Major Garrett's looking for you," he said.

The headquarters office smelled of fresh-sawn lumber. He was at his desk, and the felt armband was lying on it. "I hope you've decided to wear that."

"Yes, sir," I said. "I'll give the job my best shot."

"That's all I'm asking."

The major held out a clipboard. "This goes with the armband," he said. "Now, first thing is getting the construction cadre settled into the barracks. Giving you all pick of the beds seems a fair reward for what everybody's done. And after that..."

It was another thirty minutes before I arrived at the mess hall, late for breakfast and self-conscious about that armband I was wearing. I wondered how I'd explain it.

But Sam must have done the explaining for me. Because when I walked in, the guys started cheering. I caught friendly catcalls, and some wisecracks about how I'd have to be addressed as *Mr. Trawnley*, now, or maybe *Boss Moss*. Some shook my hand, some pounded my back, and Nate said, "Hey."

All I could think was, *Man, I hope I don't let them down.*

During the morning, we moved out of the tents. Nate and Sam, Apple, Romeo, and me, along with a half-dozen others, took up spots in B Barracks, which was nearest the mess hall. That was Apple's choice. "So we'll wake up every morning smelling breakfast."

Riley's group opted for A Barracks, which had the advantage of being a shorter walk to the rec hall.

We stored away our gear, reveling in the extra space. Maybe the long rows of double bunks, twenty to a side, would have seemed crowded to us a couple of months earlier. But after bumping knees in the tents for six weeks, we were grateful for the room.

Cal set up his phonograph, and a couple of fellows tacked up pictures of their girls. Nate set a harmonica on a shelf, next to Sam's stack of library books.

"I didn't know you played that," I said.

"Yeah, well," he said.

Then along about eleven—1100—Pops stuck his head in the door. "Time to meet the rest of CCC Company 597," he said. "The trucks are pulling in. Moss, you better get out to help the major. We just got a call that the car bringing his staff broke down. They won't make it in before tonight."

My stomach did a flip-flop. I wasn't sure I was ready to go into the junior leadership business quite so soon.

"And better move that armband to your coat," Pops said. "Guys will need to know who to look to."

A convoy of six trucks on loan from the Forest Service was already parking alongside the central field when I got to Major Garrett.

"We're going to have to play things by ear," he said.

"The roster of names is with the company sergeant. Pops told you he's been delayed?"

"Yes, sir," I answered. "So...we don't know who all the enrollees are?"

"We know where they're from. District headquarters telegraphed me their companies of origin so we wouldn't be in the total dark. Close to fifty have come from Fort Missoula, another fifty are up from a Colorado camp that didn't get winterized, and the rest are overflow from conditioning camps back east. Most all are in their first hitches.

"Oh! And I almost forgot to tell you," he added. "District did send the name of the other junior leader. It's..."

He didn't need to tell me. The cab of the first truck had already opened, and Bill Compton had got out from the passenger side.

Chapter 21

Striding up to Major Garrett, looking like he was itching to salute, he said, "Junior Leader William Compton reporting, sir."

"Welcome," the major said. "Have a good trip out?"

"It was all right, sir," Compton answered. "At least until we got to the Monroe station, and the two dozen of us from Missoula found the other hundred milling around. Their train had come in early, and they didn't have anybody in charge."

He paused as though expecting to hear who was to blame for that.

"Well," Major Garrett said, "I'm glad you got things organized. And you won't have to go it alone from here on out. I think you know my other junior leader?"

The major gestured my way, and Compton saw me for the first time. His eyes traveled to my armband, and his mouth fell open. Actually.

"But...," Compton began. His disbelief showed so clear I almost laughed out loud. I would have, except for the dose of dismay I was still struggling with. He managed a "Trawnley," and a curt nod.

The hubbub up and down the lane grew louder as guys tossed their barracks bags out of the trucks and jumped out after them. To a man, they did the same thing: hefted up their gear, got out of the way of the unloading, and then took stock of their surroundings.

It made me take a gander at the camp again, myself, trying to see what they saw. And all of a sudden the buildings that had appeared so beautiful the night before looked rough and raw. And of course there was painting still to be done, and the signs to be put up. The lane and walks to be graveled.

The major was telling Compton, "We've got Moss here to thank for having the barracks ready to move into. Without his grabbing the flag the other night, everybody would be living in tents awhile."

"Really, sir?" Compton said, giving me an unreadable glance. He nodded toward the 140 newcomers now starting to get noisy. "Shall I form them up, sir?" he asked.

"I'll do it," the major answered. "Men!" he called. He didn't shout, but talk ceased at once.

He gave a short speech of welcome, saying how they'd come to the state's third Soil Conservation Service camp. "Officially, Montana SCS-3, Company 597. Unofficially... Well, we don't have an unofficial name yet. That's something you can come up with yourselves.

"You'll be hearing a lot about your mission to help restore the land around here to a more productive condition. It'll be a big job, but anytime you get to doubting yourselves, just look around this camp to see what twenty CCC'ers can accomplish in a few weeks. And then think what one hundred sixty of you can do given several months."

Then the major introduced Compton and me. "These two are your junior leaders," he said. "They're your first link to the rest of the leadership, and they'll do their best to take care of you."

He turned to us. "Ready to take over?" he asked quietly.

Without consulting me, Compton threw him a smart, "We're ready, sir."

It caused the major to give us both a sharp glance. Then he told everybody, "Here's the day's agenda. First get settled into your new quarters. Then later in the afternoon there'll be a Christmas-tree-cutting expedition for anyone who wants to go along.

"Now, to keep things simple, I'd like those whose last names begin A through M to go with Leader Compton to A Barracks and the rest to go with Leader Trawnley to B Barracks."

I turned to Compton, who of course hadn't seen the insides of the barracks himself. "If you'd like," I offered, "I can get one of my buddies to show you—"

"No need," he said. Raising his voice, he ordered, "A Barracks men gather at the left."

Within minutes he had them moving smoothly toward their new home.

I got off to a shakier start, letters N to Z seeming to be more independent minded than the first half of the alphabet.

Or maybe it was just that I knew less what to do than Compton did.

If my guys got moved in with some order—and they did—it was because my buddies from the construction crew pitched in to help. Even Riley and T. J. Brunel came over from A Barracks to see what they could do.

"We're not needed there," Riley said. "That Compton's got things shaping up faster than a plow horse threatened with the glue factory."

And the day ended fine, with just about everybody going to get the Christmas tree.

We drove a long way to the start of some mountains, where we tromped through snow and argued about the merits of pines versus spruces versus firs, until we finally came on a tree that looked perfect.

And then we had us a grand snowball fight, A Barracks fellows against my guys, all of us dodging through the woods to ambush each other. Only Compton, ignored when he tried to lay down rules of engagement, sat it out.

We wound things up around a campfire, roasting marshmallows that Pops produced. We sang "About a Quarter to Nine," which was popular, and didn't do too bad. And then later, when long blue shadows stretched across the white forest floor, we sang "Silent Night."

"Well," Sam quietly said to me, "we've gone from being a construction cadre to being Company 597 easier than I'd have thought."

"Yeah," I agreed. "The new fellows seem like good guys."

"You did okay today."

"You think?" I asked. "I felt like it stuck out all over that I didn't know what I was doing. Especially compared to Compton."

"It did show," Sam said. "But I heard the new fellows deciding you seemed nice enough to be worth giving a chance to."

Chapter 22

Once we got past Christmas, Major Garrett and the LEMs kept us busy doing what we could around camp, as much as the snow would let us. Graveling the lane and walkways was the biggest thing, so they wouldn't turn into mud come spring.

But we also had our hands full getting ready for the dance Major Garrett had said we could hold, to celebrate the camp's completion. All Monroe would be welcome, old folks down to little kids. Of course we all hoped that whatever families came would bring daughters our own age.

Right after the New Year, on the day the last of the green paint went on the walls inside the rec center, Pops sent a bunch of us into town to post the invitations. They looked real nice, designed by a Delaware boy who got nicknamed Sketch for how he drew musical notes and such on them. The company sergeant,

Sergeant Ruffino, ran them off on his mimeograph machine.

The invitations said:

Company 597 of the CCC
invites the community of Monroe
to a dance
Saturday, January 11
7 P.M.
in the new CCC
Recreation Hall
at its camp four miles
east of town

We took them store to store, and just about all the businesspeople we asked gave us permission to put them up.

On the day of the dance itself, steam clouded the shower house all afternoon long, and guys lined up to use the ironing board. We slicked back our hair and polished our shoes. The fellows who had nice civilian slacks and shirts put them on, and the rest of us made our CCC denims look as neat as possible.

I was rummaging in my footlocker for a clean handkerchief when I remembered how Beatty gave me a box of handkerchiefs the first Christmas I knew her. It rocked me back on my heels a moment, thinking that all the dancing I'd ever done had been with Beatty as my date.

Right there on top of my socks, staring up at me, was a letter from her that had arrived the day after Christmas. I didn't have to take it out to remember what it said.

...finally wrote to your mother and she wrote back where you were. Moss, everybody here is so sorry you took off the way you did, though we understand. I'd be angry as spit, too, if I got treated like you were. Uncle Grif has put out calls to see if some other airport might not have something for you, in Texas of course, because we do miss you here...

Beatty wasn't mad at me at all. Not about me leaving without a good-bye, not over them having to find out from Ma where I'd got to.

I still hadn't written her, which was a thing I couldn't understand. Sure, at first I'd put it off because I wanted something proud to tell her, but now I had my junior leader position. That was something proud.

Only I was still putting it off.

"Hey, Moss," Apple said. "What's wrong with you? You've been staring in your locker for five minutes at least!"

"Oh!" I said, startled. "Nothing. I just..."

I had let myself get sidetracked. I grabbed the first handkerchief I saw and jammed it in my pocket.

Beatty wouldn't mind me attending the camp dance. She'd expect me to.

"I like the decorations," Maggie said, looking up at the red and green paper streamers spanning the rec hall ceiling. She and several girlfriends had been among the first to arrive, and soon after, they'd shooed her my way and then taken off in a giggling clutch.

I'd wondered about the joke they hadn't let me in on. Whatever it was, it had flustered Maggie.

She repeated her compliment about the decorations. "The room's festive," she said. "Nice and big, too."

"We moved out some of the furniture," I told her, bringing that line of talk to a dead end. Then I thought to ask, "Are your folks here?"

She answered, "No. They're home taking care of a sick cow."

"What's wrong with it?" I asked.

"Got the runs," she answered, which dead-ended that line of talk, too.

Our conversation hadn't slogged along so badly the previous times we'd met, and I wondered why it was doing so now. I was saved from the need for another go at it by the major tapping a glass for quiet.

He was wearing a fancier uniform than the one he wore on workdays, and he had with him another dressed-up officer, a captain I didn't know.

"I want to thank you all for turning out for the 597's first party," Major Garrett said. "We aim to make you as welcome here as you've made us in your community. In another month or so we'll hold an open house so you can see the plans for the conservation work we'll be doing, as well as see more of the camp than just our recreation hall. But tonight's for having fun, and I hope that's what you'll do."

He nodded toward a bosomy lady in a print dress and big hat. "Before I quit talking, I want to thank Mrs. Bessie Duvon and her trio for providing dance music for us tonight. And now, go find your partners!"

Mrs. Duvon sat down at a piano on loan from a church, and she and a pair of men with fiddles launched into a lively number. Right away people started dancing.

I recognized Mr. Schieling with a woman I guessed was his wife. Then Nate whizzed by, spinning a girl with long blond hair that streamed out behind her. I wouldn't have thought he'd know how to dance so good.

In fact, just about everybody was dancing way out of my league.

As though she'd read my mind, Maggie said, "Around here, we go to dances from the time we're babies, so we pretty much grow up knowing how." She waved toward a back corner where some women had several toddlers corralled. "Bringing the kids lets everybody come."

"Makes sense," I said.

"Do you like to dance?" she asked.

"It's okay," I said, wishing I'd let Beatty teach me more than a Texas two-step, fun though that was.

"I could show you some," Maggie offered. "If you haven't run into this brand of dancing before."

"Often as not, I've got two left feet," I told her. I looked around and spotted the refreshment table. "How about something to eat? Or a lemonade?"

Nate whirled by again and called to me, "What are you waiting for? She won't trod on your toes too much!"

And the next thing I knew, Maggie's hand was on my shoulder, and we were in motion.

It was one good party, and I probably wouldn't have left for even a short while, except for a little kid who broke free of the toddler keepers. He came careening across the dance floor, icing smeared and leading with fistfuls of squashed chocolate cupcakes.

Females all over squealed and grabbed their skirts out of his way. I made a grab for him just as Mr. Schieling swooped him up. Excited to find himself flying up into the air, the kid let loose of the cupcakes, which showered all over me.

"Oh, Moss!" Maggie sympathized, brushing off chocolate. "Your poor shirt." It had blobs of icing stuck here and there.

"I reckon I better go change," I said, and excused myself to go back to the barracks. Which was how I came to see something I'd have cause to think back on in the weeks ahead.

I was shortcutting behind the headquarters building

when I noticed there was a light on inside. Then I saw Major Garrett and the visiting officer talking to each other. What struck me odd was the look on the major's face: more...formal-like...than I was used to seeing him.

But then I spotted Maggie out on the rec hall steps, looking for me, and I put the matter out of my mind.

Sunday dawned a gloomy, snow-driven day, and most guys opted for staying inside. In the afternoon, when I took my laundry to the washhouse, I didn't see any of the staff out either, except for the major and that other officer.

With the washhouse to myself, I filled a sink with hot water, rubbed some naphtha soap into the chocolate smears on my shirt, and commenced scrubbing it against the ridges of a washboard.

The week's laundry took me a good hour, and occasionally, looking through the window above the sink, I glimpsed the two men walking from one building to another, briefly stepping inside each. It made me wonder if the visiting officer might be an inspector that the army had sent to check the construction.

I ran my rinsed clothes through the wringer and hung them to dry, and then I headed back to B Barracks, getting there just after they did. They'd paused in the doorway, looking around. Waiting for them to move, I saw it the way they did: crowded and busy and a might messy.

Several guys had pulled out personal stuff to work on

or were playing cards. Someone had strung a line between bunks near the stove and hung up several pairs
of socks. Records lay scattered across the cot nearest
Cal's phonograph.

At first no one noticed the officers. Then someone
called out, "Good afternoon, sirs," and everyone
looked up.

"Good afternoon," Major Garrett replied. "Please
carry on with what you're doing."

Then the major saw me and said, "Moss! Just the
person I was looking for! Please stop by my office
after supper."

"Yes, sir," I said. "Sure."

I glanced at the captain, wondering if he'd found a
problem somewhere that the major wanted me to have
the guys fix.

Then Major Garrett introduced me, saying, "This is
Moss Trawnley, one of the camp's junior leaders.
Moss, this is Captain Hakes."

The captain nodded. "Junior Leader," he said,
which I guessed was his idea of a greeting.

When I went over to headquarters that evening, I was
surprised to find Sergeant Ruffino and one of his cor-
porals there working. "Go on in," the sergeant told
me, waving toward the inner office.

Major Garrett was putting books into a cardboard
box. "Close the door and sit down," he said, motion-
ing me to a chair that held another half-filled carton.
"You can move that."

Sitting down himself, he studied me a moment. "Moss," he began, "I asked you in so I can give you a heads-up on some changes that are coming. As you know, I've been on temporary assignment here, detailed to get the camp built and running on an expedited schedule."

No, I thought, *I hadn't known that.*

"I'd hoped to stay on for another couple of months to complete arrangements for the camp's conservation projects and get them under way, but I'm needed at district headquarters. Captain Hakes will be taking over as commanding officer here."

Jolted—I didn't want things to change—I said, "But..." Then I stopped. I had too many protests racing through me to know which one to start with, and it wasn't my place to make them anyway. "How soon, sir?"

"As of tomorrow. I'll tell the company in the morning, but I wanted to alert you leaders first. It's important that you help keep things running while your new CO gets settled in."

"Has Captain Hakes come from another camp?" I asked.

"Nope. The CCC's as new to him as it was to you when you came on. But he's assured me he's eager to make this the best camp possible, and I'm counting on you leaders to assist him."

"I'll do my best," I promised. "But I think the 597th is already pretty good."

Major Garrett smiled. "That it is," he said, "because it's made up of a good group of young men. I've thoroughly enjoyed watching all of you pull together into a unit."

A knock sounded on the door, and Sergeant Ruffino stuck his head in. "Bill Compton is here, sir," he said.

"Tell him I'll be a few minutes more," the major said. "Moss and I are just finishing up."

When we were alone again, he said, "The camp's been fortunate to get off to a smooth start. But sooner or later problems are bound to come your way. When they do, remember you don't have to handle them by yourself.

"If it's work related, you've got the LEMs to turn to. An education adviser will be coming on board soon, and one of his jobs will be advising the enrollees about training opportunities. And fellows with personal problems can always turn to one of the chaplains who rotate in to give Sunday services."

"And the new CO," I added. "Captain Hakes. I guess he'd help."

After the slightest pause, Major Garrett said, "Yes, of course."

Chapter 23

Captain Hakes didn't waste any time letting us know camp was going to be a different place from then on. The first evening after he took over, he turned the five o'clock flag-lowering ceremony into an inspection where he picked apart everybody's appearance.

And the next day he conducted a barracks inspection a lot different from the ones the major had held. The new CO ordered pictures taken off the walls and made guys with phonographs stow them away. "Personal items can come out during free periods," he said, "but they're to be in your lockers at all other times."

Cal began, "But running the cords—"

"Don't answer back," the captain told him. "And don't speak without permission."

He continued down the barracks aisle, pausing to rip the covers off Nate's bed because the corners weren't square.

"What's your name, enrollee?" he demanded, even though LUNDGREN was plain to see on the name tag on

Nate's shirt. The captain didn't wait for an answer. "The next time I do an inspection, your bed had better be tight enough to bounce a quarter on."

Sergeant Ruffino whispered something—I caught the words "looser regulations than in the army."

Ignoring him, the captain wheeled on me. "You're the junior leader here, Trawnley," he said. "If you want to keep the position, start doing your job."

"But—"

"Didn't you hear me say not to answer back? You are first in line for responsibility for this building, and from now on it had better look as good as A Barracks looks. In fact, I think you should go see how A Barracks *does* look, and while you're there, ask Junior Leader Compton how he manages his job."

"Yes, sir," I managed. Heat was seeping up the back of my neck. He'd no call to humiliate any of us like he was doing.

"Well? What are you waiting for?" he asked. "When I say to do something, I mean to do it now!"

I felt all my guys watching me as I got my jacket and walked to the door. Most gave me looks of sympathy, and all looked bewildered or angry, or both.

Bewildered and angry. As January wore on, that description fit all of us more and more. Fellows from both barracks were like a bunch of bees whose hive had been broke into, and each new grievance set off a new round of buzzing.

Captain Hakes caused a good bit of the resentment,

when, day after day, he wanted this job and that done over. It was like nothing we did was ever quite spit and polish enough to suit.

And on top of that, little things began to go wrong. We'd been fueling the barracks stoves with coal, but when a shipment came in late, we had to make a freezing trip into the woods to get firewood. And when the coal did come, it was such a poor grade that it smoked up the room and turned the stoves filthy in no time.

Then a stew made with iffy beef gave everybody the heaves for a night.

"What happened?" I asked Romeo. We were in our bunks, curled up in misery. "Didn't anybody in the kitchen notice the meat was bad?"

"It might have smelled a tad off," he answered. "We did comment on that. But it had just come in, part of a new supply order, so we figured it had to be fresh."

But what caused the most grumbling was the lack of anything meaningful to do. Snow and cold had stopped outside work, and we'd painted about every inside wall there was to paint. The education adviser hadn't arrived yet, so we didn't have any classes to keep us busy. And the Soil Conservation Service and the army had legal work to wrap up before we could even start learning about the camp's main projects.

I couldn't blame the guys for turning to pranks, and most were harmless enough. Except Captain Hakes didn't like the ones he heard of, and when one went bad, he came down hard.

Actually, the fellows really shouldn't have taken advantage of Snooze—Wendell Perkins—like they did.

Snooze snored the loudest and slept the soundest of anyone in B Barracks, which of course was why he got the nickname he did. Anyway, one night a few guys moved him, bed and all, outside. He never even woke up till sometime later, when he got snowed on. And by then the tops of his ears were frostbit.

Another of my guys, Bo Richards, the infirmary assistant, got into an argument with Captain Hakes over whether to call the camp doctor out from town.

"I'm not wasting camp money on unnecessary medical calls," the captain said.

"He could lose the tops of his ears," Bo told him. "That might turn into a hospital stay that would cost more."

Hakes brought out the doctor, but he also took away weekend passes from everyone in B Barracks, whether we'd taken part in the prank or not.

And he gave me a dressing-down like I'd not got before. "I warned you, Trawnley. Your job is to keep the men in your barracks in line. Now that's strike one!"

Then he went on to say some more, too, mainly about how I ought to take a page from Compton's book. I didn't doubt that if Hakes could have traded me in for another Compton, he would have.

He wound up by reminding me I was being paid to represent the men in my barracks, which I hadn't done by sending Richards directly to him. "There's a chain of command for a reason. I expect you to respect it, and to see that the men in B Barracks do."

Then the last Friday in January, the military staff set off for a meeting at district headquarters, leaving Compton and me in charge of the camp.

"It's just two nights," Captain Hakes said, giving us our instructions. "The new education adviser will be arriving by train tomorrow afternoon and will give you a hand. And if you run into problems meanwhile, you can call Pops Jensen or one of the other LEMs to come out from town."

"We'll be fine, sir," Compton said.

About suppertime the temperature started to drop.

It continued plunging through the night, and I wasn't the only one who got up time and again to put on more clothes, till finally I was sleeping in my long johns, a sweater, and wool socks. I had my coat spread out on top of my blankets.

Daybreak brought pure misery. Ice coated the windows—the *inside* of the windows. You could run a finger down a wall and leave a trail through frost. And the stove had been working so hard that built-up soot had clogged the stovepipe, filling the barracks with smoke before we could get it cleaned out.

We spent the morning trying to keep the cold at bay, stuffing rags along door bottoms and putting cardboard over glass. We even took the newspapers from the rec hall and spread them under our mattresses. We got that idea from one of the New Yorkers, Leo

Swartz, who said it was a tenement-dweller's trick.
"It'll keep the cold from coming up under you so
much," he said.

"You think we ought to call Pops?" I asked Compton, who was having his own problems keeping A Barracks livable.

"What can he do?" Compton replied.

It was a fair question, and since we'd be turning
over responsibility to the new educational adviser in
just a few hours, anyway, I let the idea drop.

Compton about got his shorts in a twist deciding
which he wanted to do more—be a one-man delega-
tion to fetch the adviser from the train station or stay
in camp to run things.

"One of us has to stay, Trawnley," he said.

Finally he said, "You go. And get there on time."

Apple, watching me layer on outside gear, said,
"Where does he get off, giving you orders? You ought
to tell him you're as much a junior leader as he is."

"He's been in the job longer," I said, careful to keep
my feelings to myself. *Time in grade* was the reason
Compton gave, whenever he pulled rank on me. It was
a term he'd picked up at the military school where
he'd got his high school diploma. And where he'd
been a cadet officer, a fact he threw out whenever we
disagreed about the best way to do something.

I didn't know if *time in grade* was part of the chain
of command Captain Hakes was so big on. There was
so much I didn't know.

Apple said, "Well, I don't care how long he's been a junior leader, I can't see he's learned much except how to be almighty unpleasant."

"Him and Hakes both," Nate said. "If I'd known I'd have to answer to the likes of them, I'd have thought twice about joining up."

"Almighty unpleasant," Apple repeated, "and thick as thieves, too."

It put me in a bind, listening. On the one hand, every word of what they'd said was true. On the other, I doubted I was supposed to allow such talk.

That was one of the bad things about my job. Half the time I was flying by the seat of my pants.

"Fellows," I finally said, "it's not right to disrespect the CO. Or Bill Compton. I've got to ask you to quit."

"Actually," Sam said, "I don't think it is your job to stop Apple and Nate from saying how they feel. This isn't the army. This isn't wartime. Speech is free."

I was hurt by Sam jumping in like that. He knew more about such things than I did, and as canteen manager he had leader status himself. And here he was saying, in front of our buddies, I'd got things wrong.

"I don't have time for this," I said, grabbing up my gloves.

Nate said, "Wait. I'll drive with you."

"No need."

"Maybe not, but it's starting to snow serious out there. If drifts build up on the road, you might need a hand."

We were halfway to the garage when Sam caught up to us. He was still buttoning his coat. "Moss," he said, "don't mind what I said just now. Sometimes I don't know when to keep my mouth shut." He grimaced. "And when I do, it's the wrong time."

"You got a problem?" I asked, a mite rude I guess, but his second-guessing me rankled.

"I'm just kicking myself I didn't tell Hakes I wanted to keep my canteen job. I should have—"

"Back up," I said. "He took that away from you?"

"You didn't know?"

"No. Anyway, why? You've been running the canteen great. The guys are happy with it, and I've seen your weekly reports. They look good."

"That's why Hakes is making me take a clerking job in his office," Sam said. "I'm to help Sergeant Ruffino with his paperwork. I guess district isn't too happy with some of it."

"The sergeant does write a hand hard to read," I said, thinking how his rosters could be a chore to make out.

"Will you lose your canteen pay?" Nate asked.

"No," Sam answered. "That stays the same. It's just that as a clerk, I'll spend my days in the office. It's not what I signed onto the CCC for."

"Then you should have told him so!" Nate said.

Sam raised his eyebrows. "Isn't that what I started out saying? I don't know when to keep my mouth shut or when to open it!"

Chapter 24

I puzzled about Sam for a while, as Nate and I started into town. Sam was a hard one to figure. He had all this education the rest of us didn't have—a way of talking and knowing things that said his growing up had been pretty different from ours.

Like he'd come from a family with money and schooling.

But he'd never said so—at least not beyond mentioning his father worked in New York, when another Boston kid asked what Mr. Whitney did.

I'd thought to myself, that must be some job for Mr. Whitney to travel back and forth so far. Or maybe Sam had just said the first thing that came to mind, to avoid embarrassment.

He never read aloud anything from the letters he got.

Then Nate's sliding the truck into a snowbank drove Sam from my mind. "Couldn't help it," Nate said, as he pulled out shovels. "The road's getting worse by the minute."

The third time we got stuck, he said, "I really don't care for the looks of this."

"You think the weather's going to get worse?" I asked.

"It might. We'd be smart to pick up the adviser and get ourselves turned around as fast as we can."

The person we'd gone to pick up didn't get off the train. No one did. And after Nate and I discussed what to do, I got the stationmaster to put through a telephone call to Pops.

"Don't worry about it," Pops said. "You boys drive back to camp while you still can, and the missus or I'll check trains till the new man shows up. He can stay the night with us if need be."

I couldn't have said how Nate and I made the drive back to camp, except Nate knew how to lay on the gas going downhill, and he kept the accelerator floored when I'd have been pumping the brake pedal. We slipped and slid and fishtailed till I thought the back half of the truck might disconnect from the front.

But I had to hand it to Nate. He got us to the 597th in one piece. Actually, I had to give Nate credit for even finding the camp. By the time we reached the entrance, snow had hidden the lane into it and made the buildings almost invisible.

"We ought to string some safety lines," Nate said. "This is becoming the kind of blizzard a body can get lost in."

I took Nate's suggestion to Compton, who argued that we didn't have authorization to make the camp into a spiderweb.

I bit back what I wanted to ask: *Do you need permission for getting up in the morning? For blowing your nose?*

"We don't have to do the whole camp," I said. "But we need to make sure guys can at least get between the barracks and the mess hall without getting lost."

"I can't believe the situation is going to get that bad," he said. "And I don't know what we'd use for line, anyway."

"There's some spools of cable left from camp construction."

Compton, scanning the slanting snowfall from the A Barracks steps, appeared undecided. Then a swirl of snow wrapped us, so that for a moment I couldn't see him and likely he couldn't see me.

"Get the men on it if you're going to, and don't forget to run a line over here," he said. "But it's your responsibility."

I had a crew attaching one end of a cable line to the mess hall door when it dawned on me why Compton hadn't wanted to run the operation himself. He didn't want the blame if Hakes returned and disapproved of the lines as an unnecessary precaution.

But that, anyway, wasn't going to happen.

The blizzard moved in full force while we were eating supper, and the only way fellows got back to their barracks was by hanging on to the lines we'd strung. Without them, a guy could have walked within a couple of feet of a building and not even seen the lights inside, visibility was so poor.

"How long do you think this will last?" I asked Nate.

"Till it's over," he answered. Then he laughed, probably at how dismayed I must have looked. "Likely it'll end by morning."

He was wrong about that. Snow continued piling up through the night and into Sunday. Then, in the middle of the afternoon, the air suddenly stilled and the sky turned bright blue.

By then, though, the camp was a rolling plain of white, with low spots filled in and drifts reaching to roof edges. Wind had pushed the snow into parallel lines over the central field, making it look like a vast washboard. The canvas tops of trucks sagged under the snow's weight.

Telephone and electric lines were down, but we didn't need a phone call to know Captain Hakes and his staff wouldn't make it back that day.

"Think we'll get plowed out soon?" I said to Nate, hoping he'd have encouraging news about how the Monroe area handled blizzards.

"Don't hold your breath," he answered. "The county's forever short on equipment, and what there is will be plowing out highways, not poking back here."

Compton and I consulted, or, anyway, he let me know his mind. "I've already checked with the kitchen," he said. "There's food enough, so that's not a problem. It's up to us to keep things running in the captain's absence, just as if he were here."

"There's a pipe busted in the B Barracks latrine," I said. "I shut the water off and aim to get a crew fixing it."

"Don't try, if there's a chance you'll make things worse."

I gave him a look before heading off.

"I mean it, Trawnley," he called.

Of course we got the pipe fixed okay. After all, the group of us who'd been on the construction cadre had installed it to begin with, and it felt right good to be working with wrenches and such again.

As we worked, though, I occasionally caught Nate staring out a window, chewing on his lower lip.

"Problem?" I asked.

"Just wishing I was home. Dad and Maggie will be having a time getting feed to any stock that got caught out in the fields."

"The animals won't come to the barn on their own?"

"They might not be able to," he said. "It depends on how deep the snow is, where they are, and on how much the cold has sapped their strength."

"But they'll survive?"

"Depends," he said again.

"On how soon they get food?"

"On that, and on when this cold breaks. When it's down twenty or thirty below like this, it's tough on creatures."

The temperature fell even further Sunday night. Too uncomfortable to sleep, I huddled in my bed and tried to think how I could describe such cold to Beatty.

The best I could come up with was to tell her to think about the difference between a morning just chilly enough for frost to form and a day when heat shimmered above the airport tarmac.

I'd tell her to imagine that same difference, only this time to subtract sixty or seventy degrees from the freezing point instead of adding to it.

Lately I'd been doing that: trying to think how I could explain this or that about Montana to Beatty.

Or, if it was a Texas thing that crossed my thoughts, how I might explain it to Maggie.

I kept the girls in two opposite corners of my mind, where I didn't have to explain them to each other. It wasn't the best arrangement, but truth be, I didn't want either of them to move out.

Which was maybe one reason, anyway, why I still hadn't written to Beatty.

Monday morning, which was still bitter cold, I was out with a shoveling crew when a bulky figure appeared on the lane into camp. I looked and looked again, because he seemed to be walking on top of the snow.

Then, when he got closer, I saw the long snowshoes that he swung wide with each stride. I'd never seen any before, and immediately I wished I had some.

"Where's the camp commander?" he asked us, his words muffled by a thick scarf wound around his face.

I explained about the staff being gone. "I'm one of the junior leaders," I said. "Can I help?"

"Owen Schieling says you've a bulldozer out here. We need you boys to open up some of the back roads so folks can get to their livestock."

"Sure," I said. "We've got a dozer for the conservation work we'll be doing. But I don't know as anybody knows how to operate it yet."

"I probably can," a usually quiet fellow named Swen Amonson volunteered. "My dad does roadwork and has shown me some."

"A lot of folks will be grateful," the man said. "I'm Les Rinehert, by the way. I have a farm and a stranded band of sheep, myself."

We got keys from the rack inside the maintenance shop and were firing up the bulldozer when Compton appeared. "What do you think you're doing?" he demanded.

I explained, expecting he'd leap to help, but instead he said, "Captain Hakes didn't leave us permission to use the equipment, or the gasoline that it will need." He turned to the farmer. "You'll have to come back when our CO returns and ask him."

Mr. Rinehert gave Compton a look like he wondered what kind of fool he was dealing with. By the time the road was open enough for the CO to get in, our bulldozer wouldn't be needed.

"Look," I told Compton, "these people have got an emergency. We have to do what we can."

"No," he said. "I already told you we don't have the authority to send out equipment." He again told Mr. Rinehert, "Come back when Captain Hakes is here."

The farmer's face, what I could see of it above his scarf and below his cap, turned a mottled red. "I'll take the dozer myself if I need to," he said.

"You won't need to," I told him. I turned to Swen, who'd stopped his efforts to start the engine. "Go ahead," I said. "Crank it up."

"Don't," Compton ordered him.

Swen looked from him to me, hesitated, and then reached for the choke.

"Don't worry," I told Compton, who looked fit to be tied. "I'll take responsibility."

"You can count on that," he said. "I'll make sure the captain knows just what happened, because I am not going to take the blame when he has to report how camp equipment and materials got used without his say-so, and maybe damaged." He jerked his head toward Swen. "How do you even know he can run that thing?"

I turned to Mr. Rinehert. "We also have stake trucks and lots of fellows who can swing shovels. We'll do whatever we can."

Farmers and ranchers came out to meet us at place after place. They were bundled up as heavy as we were, so I never did see a face—just eyes squinting against the bright sun bouncing off snow.

They'd fall into line behind us, driving their horse-drawn wagons loaded with hay and grain. Swen led the way, breaking through the snow with the dozer blade.

Then came the trucks full of CCC'ers. When we got near a set of animals a bunch of us would scramble out and shovel a path through the snowbank, till a fence stopped us.

Then a wagon would maneuver in and a farmer would toss out food.

Mostly, just seeing hay was enough to get the animals to push their way to it. But there was one place where a dozen or so cows didn't have enough oomph left to get on their feet and walk even the twenty yards that would save their lives.

"We could cut the fence and dig a path to them," I suggested.

But the man whose place it was didn't wait for that. With snowshoes on his feet, he stepped over the fence, hurried to the closest cow, and grabbed onto her head. And he pulled and yelled and pulled and patted her behind her ears. It was the dangest thing. Sad like.

Right till suddenly the cow got to its knees and then heaved itself upright. It staggered to a mound of hay, ate some, and then mooed loudly. And then the rest of those animals started struggling to stand.

Swen had idled back the dozer motor by then, and the rest of us leaned on our shovel handles till we saw the last of the cows reach the food.

The man in the field moved from one to another, talking to them and patting each like it was a saved child. Then he came back to us. "Thanks," he said. "You boys saved their lives. I'll remember."

Chapter 25

Captain Hakes and his staff rolled in the next day, and almost at once Compton and I got word he wanted us in his office.

Compton strode beside me, tight-lipped and angry. "I'm not letting myself get dragged down by this, Trawnley," he said. "I don't care how you explain the gallons of fuel you good as gave away, or that truck with the smashed fender. Just make it clear I had nothing to do with it."

"Don't worry," I said. "I will."

Sergeant Ruffino waved us into the CO's office, where Captain Hakes finished reading something at his desk. Then he said, "I understand the road plowing required eighty gallons of gasoline, and one of the stake trucks will need some repairs. Is that correct?"

"Yes, sir," I said. "The—"

The captain didn't let me finish. "The expenditures and the need for repairs are unfortunate."

Compton broke in. "Sir," he said, "Leader Trawnley clearly understood—"

Hakes frowned at the interruption, but Compton went on, "I just want you to know, sir, that I didn't—"

"However," the captain continued, "the CCC is charged with helping meet emergencies when it can, and with doing what's reasonable to earn goodwill in the communities where we put our camps. That was, in fact, the subject of the meeting that my staff and I just attended. And, fortunately, word of your activities here reached us while we were still in discussion."

Compton threw me a swift glance. His thoughts must have been bouncing around fast as a pinball snapped too hard.

Captain Hakes said, "The storm provided the 597th's first opportunity to show the people of Monroe that we're here to help. I'm most pleased that in my absence you seized the initiative."

Before I could get a word in edgewise, Compton jumped in.

"Thank you, sir," he said. "As the more senior leader, I made the decision I believed you'd have made." He gave me a patronizing smile. "And Leader Trawnley eventually came around, too, to my way of thinking."

Compton kept going, shameless as a dog looking you in the eye while plotting to steal your supper. "And he was quite a help directing the men," he said.

I was too dumbfounded for speech.

And then the moment to say anything passed, as Captain Hakes reached for his paperwork. "That will be all," he said.

Then he added, "Leader Compton, I'm glad to know I can count on your good judgment."

"Why'd you say what you did?" I demanded, as soon as Compton and I were beyond earshot of headquarters.

He walked on for several paces without answering. Then he gave me that same smile he'd flashed back in Hakes's office, and angled off toward A Barracks.

I was so mad I could have walked out of the camp and not looked back, but I kept it from the fellows.

Hearing how Compton had taken credit that belonged to just about everybody in the camp *but* him would take the shine off of how good they were feeling about themselves.

Also, I didn't want it to get about how I'd let myself be taken advantage of. Compton couldn't have pulled the wool over Hakes's eyes if I hadn't let him. The fellows didn't need to know they had a leader not even able to take care of himself.

So Sam caught me by surprise that evening, when he said, "You should have told the CO that if Compton had had his way, the roads around here still wouldn't be plowed."

"How do you know I didn't?"

"I overheard Hakes tell Sergeant Ruffino to make a note in Compton's file about his initiative. Hakes wants to remember to mention it in the recommendation he's going to write for when Compton's hitch is up."

"Recommendation for what?"

"West Point."

"Compton wants to go there?"

"Apparently. And Hakes is all for it."

"Is Hakes a West Pointer?"

"No. But he's a career soldier, and all for anything that will help his career. Including recruiting."

I told Sam, "I guess if Compton's aiming to run the army, we better be glad the Great War's behind us."

"There'll be others," Sam said.

"No," I told him. "That was the war to end wars. I studied that in school."

"And you believe it?" he said. Count on Sam to be ready to debate a point.

Well, better that than go on about how I ought to handle Compton.

I was just thankful Compton and I didn't have much cause to cross paths in the coming days, except at the captain's briefing sessions. And there, the captain would just mostly run down the next day's plans and Compton would snap out *Yes, sir* like he'd personally see the plans got carried out.

Though when something didn't go just right, he'd find a way to make it sound like my doing.

"You ought to fight back," Sam said more than once. Working in the headquarters office, he heard most of what went on.

"I guess," I always answered.

But I didn't know how, and that was a lack in me. I thought once or twice about talking things over with Pops, but I couldn't bring myself to do it. Asking for advice would have meant admitting I wasn't sure what I was doing.

Anyway, about then we entered a time when Compton and I were too busy helping the military staff organize our guys to get in each other's way.

As soon as the weather warmed up some—if you could call going from thirty below to three above warming up—we had us our hands full digging out the rest of the camp.

And we ferried hay up into the mountains to a Fish and Wildlife crew trying to keep an antelope herd from starving. Sam reported that the CO dithered about that one, trying to decide what district would think.

Apple asked, "Why can't he do a job just because it needs doing?"

Sam answered, "Sergeant Ruffino says Hakes is bucking for a promotion and is weighing everything against that."

"What I'd like," Apple said, "is to promote him out of here! What's he want to be promoted to?"

"To major, of course," Nate said. That's what comes after captain.

"And out of here, too," Sam added. "The sergeant said Hakes thinks the CCC's a career dead end."

Myself, I didn't much care *why* the captain okayed work like the hay delivery. It kept the fellows busy and content during the day.

Chapter 26

Keeping them occupied in the hours after supper was trickier. They'd begun complaining they could play just so much Ping-Pong, and that Thursday movie night only rolled around on Thursdays. Even the newsreels about the winter Olympics going on in Germany were wearing thin. Adolf Hitler had opened them, to a great big cheering crowd.

And as for using their free time to write letters—well, it seemed like the mail didn't bring anything anybody wanted to answer.

One Saturday Sam got a note from home that made him purple up in rage.

"I do *not* have asthma," he exclaimed.

"What are you talking about?" I asked.

"Just...nothing!" he answered.

But that evening, he told me a story he said he didn't want getting around. I wouldn't have spread it anyway.

"You want to know why I never write home?" he asked.

"I guess you don't like letter writing any more than me," I answered.

"My mother asked me not to write. She doesn't want the postman seeing letters coming from a CCC camp."

"I don't get it," I said.

"Do you know what it's like to have somebody ashamed of you?"

I waited.

"My mother doesn't want people knowing I'm doing relief work, even though she suggested the CCC, to get me out of Boston when we couldn't keep paying for my school there. She's told all her friends I'm in New Mexico for my health. First it was allergies, and now it's asthma!"

I had to say something. I settled on: "Lots of us have dropped out of high school. We'll go back when we can."

"Not me. I'm done with school. I told them that when they didn't want me going to a public one."

Sam, the most logical guy in the company—the guy who used his afternoons in town to go to the *library*, for crying out loud—wasn't making much sense.

I guessed he was just talking out of bitterness, so I said, "You ought to rethink that."

"I didn't ask what you think!" he snapped.

I started to turn away, but that didn't seem the right thing to do. "What about your dad?" I finally asked. "Didn't you say he had a job in New York?"

"Right," Sam answered. "He sells hot chestnuts from a Manhattan street stand. Then once a month he rides a boxcar home to Boston, changes into a suit, and walks around looking prosperous for everybody to see."

"Gosh," I said. "I'm sorry."

"I didn't tell you to get sympathy," Sam said. "It's just...sometimes I feel as if I'm boiling over inside. And...and sometimes I just hate them."

I could have said it right then. I could have told Sam the whole story about Pa. It still boiled up in me when I was least looking for it to. When I'd messed up on one thing or another, especially.

But I couldn't bring myself to let even Sam know.

"You'll work it out," I told him.

He just looked at me. Whatever he'd needed, it had been more than that.

It was one more time I could have walked away from my job, walked away from the camp and all its problems, and not looked back.

The mail did bring a lot of problems.

A whole raft of fellows got Dear Johns from girls tired of long-distance romances.

I got another letter from Beatty, a chatty catch-up on airport doings. An additional flight in each direction was going in and out each day. Kenzie, the mechanic I'd worked with, had finally retired. *I know you're busy. Write when you can.*

Not a Dear John at all, but its own kind of problem, since I still hadn't written her.

And a Brooklyn kid named Melvin received notification that his little brother had been sent to a different foster home. I couldn't do much for Mel except help him read the long words.

Well, read almost all the words. Mel hadn't ever gone to school but for a couple of years.

It made me wish the camp's education adviser would get to work before all our hitches ended.

The man Nate and I went to pick up the weekend of the blizzard had got only as far as Butte before telegraphing the CCC that no paycheck in the world was worth living in Montana in the winter.

And then when his replacement, a Mr. Romsteder, had arrived, he'd settled into the education building quiet as a barn cat slipping into a kitchen.

About all he did was post a sign-up sheet for appointments so we could talk over where we were, educationwise, and put up a bulletin board with the question WHAT DO YOU WANT TO LEARN? Under it, he put class suggestions that ran from GREAT WORKS OF LITERATURE to PRACTICAL MATHEMATICS.

"What?!" Apple said. "He expects us to volunteer to go to school nights? In our free time? I'd sooner watch grass grow."

That was pretty much everybody's attitude, despite all the griping about how there wasn't anything to do.

"It doesn't have to be a school class," Sam said. "I heard him talking with Captain Hakes about how he'll try to provide whatever we want, though academics is certainly a possibility."

Sam sounded pretty excited, for a guy who'd declared school was behind him.

"What I want is some time away from here, preferably with a sweet girl," someone said, and of course after that whatever point Sam had been trying to make got lost in the fellows' carryings-on. Girls were a distracting topic, always.

Later on, though, when it was just him and me talking, Sam said the conversation he'd overheard had been Captain Hakes chewing Mr. Romsteder out, as much as anything.

"I think Mr. Romsteder wants to put together a good program," Sam said. "But Hakes wants it all done right away—everybody signed up for something—so the numbers on this month's report to district will look good."

"That again!" I said. I was getting sick and tired of how everything kept coming down to Hakes's wanting to put on a good show. "Still, I hope Mr. Romsteder pulls it off, for the fellows' sakes."

It looked less and less like he would, though, as the days went by with hardly anybody signing up for his classes. Despite how Compton and I harangued on everybody, after Hakes good as ordered us to.

Then an idea kind of fell down out of the sky.

It came one evening when I was in the barracks darning socks. Most of the fellows were over to the rec hall, and several of the ones who weren't were singing along with Stan Worden and Jimmy O'Neill on their guitars and Nate on his harmonica.

They got to the end of a piece, and Hal Linchfeld, who had a right good voice, asked, "Anybody know 'Aloha Oe'?"

Nate and Jimmy shook their heads.

Stan said, "Me, either. But I may have the music."

He dug into his locker and came out with some sheet music he paged through. "I do have it," he said, picking out the beginning of a tune on his guitar strings. "Here's the melody."

Jimmy looked astounded. "You play by dots?" he said. "I never knew anybody could do that."

"I had to learn how to," Stan said, never missing a beat. "My ear's not so good as yours."

He went back over some notes he hadn't got quite right the first time before adding, "And there's nothing in the books that tells me how to play the chords you do. I'd give anything to know those."

"The grass is always greener, huh?" Hal said. "Here I can sing, but what I'd like is to play a harmonica."

"Stan and Hal are nice guys," Sam said quietly.

"Yeah," I answered. "They all are."

A little later I walked over to the lighted education building.

Knocking and opening the door at the same time, I caught a glimpse of Mr. Romsteder at his desk, just staring at a pile of papers. Looking up, he took a second to refocus. Then, his face brightening, he said, "Moss Trawnley, right? Come in." He waved to a chair. "Take a seat."

He seemed so tickled to have company, I felt bad saying I couldn't stay long. And now I was there, I didn't know how to get started. "How's it going?" I asked.

"Fine, fine," he answered. Then he said, "No, that's not true. You're one of the few enrollees who've found this building, and I can't understand it. The CCC is offering such an opportunity, whatever anyone wants to learn..."

He glanced at the papers on his desk. "And some of these boys need so much. A few can't even read. Others ought to be in college, and I could at least give them something to keep their minds growing. I just can't understand why there's no interest."

Hoping he wouldn't take offense—after all, I was about to again stick my oar in when I hadn't been asked—I told him about Stan, who could read music but didn't know much about playing his guitar, and about Jimmy, who could only play what he'd heard or felt. About Hal, who wanted to play harmonica, and about Nate, who could play his so sweet it made a body want to cry.

I said, "I was thinking maybe you might set up a class where they could teach each other, along with anybody else who wants to sit in. I know it wouldn't be real school stuff, but they'd be learning something, which would be better than lying around grousing all the time, which is becoming a real problem, and—"

I broke off because I hadn't meant the suggestion to sound like I was asking for help.

In no time, knocking on doors around Monroe, Mr. Romsteder rounded up an assortment of beat-up instruments that played pretty good despite their looks, and the 597th got a band going. Everyone was welcome, even the ones who stuck to shakers and drumming on upside-down trash cans.

Then T. J. Brunel allowed as how he'd done some leather tooling, and that led to several fancy belts getting started and even one saddle.

One of the LEMs offered to teach engine repair to anybody interested, and Apple jumped on that.

A dozen guys, including Melvin, began quietly attending a basic reading class, and if anybody thought it was funny seeing seventeen- and eighteen-year-olds toting around second-grade readers, they didn't say.

And before I knew what happened, Mr. Romsteder had me teaching a dozen guys the Morse code and explaining how radios worked.

That was Tuesday nights. Mondays and Wednesdays, he had Sam and me in his Great Works of Literature

class. We were reading *Hamlet,* a fellow with some
family problems worse than ours.

And Sam was taking a couple of other courses, too,
to earn his high school diploma.

Of course, Mr. Romsteder got a nickname: *Teach.*
More than one guy said he was the nicest teacher
they'd ever run into, once you got past his shyness.

The only person unhappy with the program was
Compton. His nose was out of joint because Mr.
Romsteder had told Captain Hakes whose idea the
music program was.

"Don't let it go to your head," Compton told me.
"The captain knows even losers get things right once
in a while."

Part III

Part III

Chapter 27

Meanwhile, we'd got our first look at the conservation work ahead of us.

I'd been so occupied with the day-to-day doings of the camp and with trying not to annoy Hakes more than I could help, I'd pretty much put the camp's mission out of my mind. But now it came back to me, the reason I was in the CCC beyond needing the job.

The way Pops explained things, we were going to demonstrate a bunch of ways to stop farm erosion in its tracks and also put some really sick land to good use.

He unrolled a map and pointed to a spot in the center of it. "This is a plot that reverted back to the government after a string of homesteaders gave up on it, and it's as good an example of all that's wrong as you'll find anywhere."

Turning to the chalkboard, he said, "Right now it looks something like this." He drew a square and then sketched in some bluffs and a small creek.

"I've been around long enough to remember when that was a pretty stream," he said, "but these days it's naked as a jaybird. Just about every shrub and tree that ever grew along it was cut down, plowed under, or killed by grazing. It dries up most summers and silts up when it doesn't."

"Silts up?" someone asked.

"Fills with dirt that washes into it when the gullies run full."

Then Pops drew a rough oval over a portion of his picture. "And this," he said, "is what's going to keep you fellows earning your keep."

"A lake?" someone guessed.

"More like a pond," he answered. "Just a couple of acres of reservoir. But that's big enough to help get control over the erosion that stripped stream is causing. And it—and the land around it—will be a place where wildlife can make a comeback. Birds, especially, which will help with grasshoppers."

"So...how do you make a pond?" someone asked. "Just dig it?"

"We'll do some digging," Pops answered. "But we'll mainly follow the contours of the land, deepening a natural basin that's already there. The bank on one side will need to be built up. And an earthen dam will go on the lowest side, along with a small concrete spillway.

"We'll plant willows and other shrubs along all the

banks to help hold the soil in place and invite those birds in."

Someone said, "It sounds like a lot of work to go to, to kill a few bugs."

I glanced around, sure it had to be a city fellow talking, and I was right.

Pops told him, "If you'd ever seen a grasshopper army eat through a whole wheat field in just hours, you wouldn't be saying that. Besides, the camp's projects are about a lot more than grasshoppers." He glanced at his watch. "But right now, it's time for lunch. Afterwards, there'll be a fellow in from the Soil Conservation Service to tell you about that."

Most of the guys left for the mess hall, but a few, including Nate and me, hung around to study the map and drawing. Nate told Pops, "I know that land. It abuts ours on the west side."

"That it does," Pops said. "I didn't have anything to do with choosing it, but I'm glad your folks will be among those to benefit. The reservoir should cut down on flooding from spring runoff and make for more reliable irrigation, too."

"What worries me," Nate said, "is whether that reservoir will leave any water coming down the creek for us to draw on."

"You needn't fret," Pops said. "The reservoir's not going to be all that deep, and once it's filled, then water will go over the spillway right into the creek bed and on through your place, same as always."

"Do you think our project might really help your folks?" I asked Nate, on our way to lunch.

"I suppose. But if I know my dad, it's going to have to be working before he'll admit it might. And it's not like he'll be able to ignore the reservoir meanwhile, since he'll see the construction every time he goes outside."

Then Nate grinned. "But I can tell you this. Maggie's going to be all for it."

Mr. Caldwell, an engineer with the Soil Conservation Service, spoke to us in the afternoon. He said he'd be our project superintendent—not working with us every day, but taking overall responsibility for what we did.

"As soon as the ground thaws we'll begin digging," he told us. "But first I've got another task I'd like you to tackle.

"The way I see it, one of the toughest jobs in front of us will be getting folks to understand what we're doing and why. Otherwise, we won't get people to try our ideas on their own places.

"I've got pamphlets that explain it all, but it's been my experience that until a person sees a thing, he's not likely to grasp it fully. So I want you to build some models that will show both the reservoir we're going to put in and also a variety of conservation practices."

"What will we make the models out of?" someone asked.

"Whatever you want. How you do it is up to you. I'll just show you the things I'd like included."

"How big?" another asked.

"Your call, too," Mr. Caldwell said. "But make them big enough that details like irrigation gates can be shown. And big enough to hold a discussion around."

For the reservoir, we covered a couple of broad planks with chicken wire shaped to show the basin and how the land would be once we got done moving earth around. Then we covered that with pulped newspapers—*papier-mâché*, Sam called it—that we painted blue for water and buff for dirt.

And then we got to work on details.

Using twigs for trunks and tufts of dried moss for leaves, we made tiny trees that we put in a quadruple line along the windward side of the reservoir to form a shelterbelt. Littler bits of moss and grass became willow bushes that we glued on all the banks.

We made another model just of the dam, a long earthen berm broken in the middle by a smallish concrete spillway and control gate.

Nate took charge of a model of a farm where everything was done conservationwise. Strips of fallow land—land at rest—alternated with strips of various crops like wheat that drew from the soil, and also with cover crops like clover that Mr. Caldwell said were good for putting nutrients back in.

Sketch came up with the idea of mixing dirt into plaster of paris to make a paste we could rake with a fork to show plow lines.

Plow lines were a big thing. Mr. Caldwell had us show them following the curves of the land. "With contour plowing, rain is caught crosswise by the plants and held instead of being left free to run off between rows."

"Those wavy rows look like they were made by someone who couldn't walk straight," Apple said, which was just what I was thinking. In my growing-up days of walking behind a plow mule, the biggest compliment my pa could pay me was to say my rows were straight as the teeth on a comb.

"That may be," Mr. Caldwell told Apple, "but they'll conserve water and topsoil both."

"I guess what you're saying makes sense," Apple said. Despite his jokes, he was taking this dead serious.

Just like Nate was.

Most guys thought Nate's model was a pretend farm, but I recognized the layout of the tiny structures he put on it: house, barn, outbuildings. "That's your place, isn't it?" I asked him.

He nodded. "You think Dad will recognize it?"

"Bound to," I said.

I had to respect Nate's effort. Probably the shortest route he could take to getting clear of his folks' farm would be to let it go under, but he was trying hard as his sister to not let that happen. I watched him put a windbreak around the house and put in channels for an irrigation system. He even painted a small flower garden.

"It's right pretty," I said.

He shrugged. "I guess," he said. "But *pretty's* not going to sell my dad."

Chapter 28

Having real work to do charged up the guys. That and the prospect of that open house the major had promised the town. We'd rather have had another dance, but a social occasion was a social occasion.

When warm chinook winds in early March melted the last of the snow, we were able to spruce up the camp's outsides. We made signs for buildings, washed all the vehicles, and raked the graveled lanes smooth.

We even built a monument at the camp's entrance, out of rocks held together with concrete made from cement Mr. Schieling gave us. He'd overheard fellows in town discussing what kind of entry marker we might make, and suggested using rocks.

We built it about five feet high, in the shape of the sheepherders' monuments that stood atop hilltops here and there. Nate said they were from when folks ran sheep in a big way, and the bands would be put in the charge of herders, who sometimes built rock piles just to pass the time.

"We ought to give our camp a real name," Apple said, as we finished up. "Remember how Major Garrett said we should think one up?"

"What I'll remember about this place is that it's where I lived through the coldest days of my life," said Bo Richards, a Georgia fellow. "I never thought forty degrees would seem balmy, but after what January and February threw at us…"

He got a laugh, and he'd given us our name. *Cold Day Camp*. A couple of the guys volunteered to make a wood sign board, to put next to the monument.

"Guess we're done here, then," I said.

"Almost," Apple said. Hunkering down, he used a stick to put a neat set of initials—E. D.—in the wet mortar.

"Why don't you just write *Apple*?" someone asked. "That's how we all know you."

"'Cause it's a nickname that could be anybody's," Apple answered. "I'm kind of proud of this camp we've built, and of the work we're going to do, and I want it official. I had a hand."

There wasn't any need for more talk. One after another, we put our initials into the monument, until there were two columns of them wandering down between the stonework.

Sam went last and added the year: *1936*.

We put up the sign with our new name the morning of the open house, and folks got a kick out of seeing COLD DAY CAMP. And it fit. Another bout of cold temperatures had replaced the chinooks.

Captain Hakes didn't much like the sign, but it was too late for him to order it taken down. Anyway, he was busy shaking hands with all our visitors and taking congratulations on how nice the camp looked.

Just about all Monroe had turned out, just like it had for our dance. This time, though, women and kids mainly gathered around refreshments in the mess hall, while men gravitated to the project models we'd set up in the rec hall.

With exceptions, of course. A reporter from the *Monroe Herald* was busy as a june bug on a May day, buzzing about with his camera and notepad. I saw Sam glom on to him and wondered why.

And Maggie stayed right at her father's elbow, so intent on understanding the project models that she reminded me of Beatty, peering into the nose of an airplane.

Mr. Caldwell was there to explain it all. "Using strip farming, contour plowing, and regular rotation of soil-depleting crops with soil-maintaining and soil-building ones, you will not only stop wearing out your land, you will start improving it."

"How about that back section along the old wagon road?" asked Mr. Lundgren, who'd caught on right away it was his own place he was looking at.

"It's not suitable for cultivation," Mr. Caldwell said. "There's no way to irrigate it in the dry season, and the slope is too steep not to need permanent sod anchoring it. When you persist in trying to farm land like that, you feed dust storms and invite erosion."

"No," Mr. Lundgren said. "That's not true. Back when we were getting decent rain—"

Maggie tugged on his arm and whispered, "Dad, just listen, please."

She got looks from some of the other men like if she was their daughter, she'd know her place. One of them muttered, "I don't know which is worse, a bunch of wet-behind-the-ears Roosevelt pups telling us what to do, or a female."

Mr. Caldwell flushed. "At fifty, I'm hardly what you'd call a pup. And if you mean these CCC'ers, you just wait and see what they're going to accomplish."

Eyes turned to Mr. Lundgren, who hesitated a moment. Then he took Maggie's elbow and moved her in for a closer look.

I had to admire him for it, and, seeing Nate's expression, I suspicioned he was proud, too.

Then Mr. Caldwell ended any pretending that the model was a make-believe place. "Mr. Lundgren," he said, "your son knows every foot of your holdings, and he helped come up with this plan.

"It uses your water resources well, it puts crops where they're most likely to succeed, and it returns to natural growth a part of the prairie that should never have been plowed up. I'm asking you to give it a try."

"Even if I wanted to," Mr. Lundgren said, "I couldn't afford it."

"There's government money available to mitigate the expense of making changes."

"Just for him?" someone asked, and got told no.

"There's a plan for reimbursing anybody who switches acreage out of soil-depleting crops, or who puts in such things as shelterbelt trees. We'll even *get* you the trees," Mr. Caldwell said.

I was watching Mr. Lundgren.

He appeared uncertain, like he didn't know if he was being offered a gift or tempted with disaster wrapped up like one.

Then all of a sudden he looked straight at me. "You believe this will work?" he asked.

I wished he'd picked on someone else, but I answered. "Mr. Caldwell says it will, and Pops Jensen and the other LEMs think so."

"I'm asking you," Mr. Lundgren told me. "You grew up on a farm. What do you believe?"

"Louisiana's different from here," I said, while my mind raced ahead, picking my next words. I could feel Maggie and Nate willing me to say the right thing.

"But I've seen a lot of what's not working, all the way from there across Texas and up," I said. "I think farmers and ranchers have got to find new ways of doing things, and I don't know how better than to listen to folks who've studied it all scientifically."

I glanced at Nate.

"At colleges," I added.

Ignoring that last, Mr. Lundgren pinned me down, "So you're for it?"

I didn't want to answer more directly. I didn't want

him resting any part of such a big decision on my say-so, and it seemed preposterous that he might. I didn't know the first thing about farming in country like this.

But Maggie and Nate were staring at me, their eyes begging, *Say yes, Moss.*

Reluctantly, I nodded.

And after a moment, Mr. Lundgren nodded back. "Well, you've already shown me you've got good sense."

Maggie started to say something, but Nate caught her eye and motioned that she should leave well enough alone.

The three of us slipped away, just after Mr. Lundgren said to Mr. Caldwell, "Now, if I *was* to go along…"

Outside, Nate thanked me, though his voice was a bit stiff. I couldn't blame him for having mixed feelings. Mr. Lundgren was considering the project, just like Nate had wanted, but he'd asked me instead of his own son for an opinion.

"You're the one who made the model so good," I said.

"Yeah," he answered. "And I'm the one who wants to go off to college and become one of those scientists." He glanced from me to his sister. "Look, why don't you two go for a walk if you want. I'll see you later."

Maggie and I took the long way around, along a path that ran behind the mess hall. When we were out of sight of everybody she suddenly threw her arms around me. Just brieflike, but I knew I'd been hugged.

"Dad's going to go for it," she said. "He will, I just know it, and it will be your doing, and—" She broke off with a sharp, "Moss, watch out—"

Down the path came waddling the best-fed skunk I had ever seen, right toward us. It wasn't skunklike behavior at all, and the two of us started backing up, though Maggie was giggling.

"That must be Thief!" she said, as the skunk climbed the steps to the kitchen.

"Who? The skunk?" I asked. The back door opened, and Romeo set down a bowl of something that the animal lit right into.

"Romeo," I called, "you better be careful."

"So far he hasn't sprayed anybody I know of," he replied, coming down to join us. "And he's been visiting regular for a couple of weeks now. And reforming fast. He hardly ever steals anything without first giving me a chance to offer it to him."

Thief was a dainty eater, I had to hand him that. He picked up each piece of food and examined it carefully before popping it into his mouth. Except for what looked like a fish skin. That went in in one fast motion.

And he didn't smell too bad, for a skunk.

"You can pet him if you want," Romeo said. "Though you might want to wait till he's done."

"Oh, I think I can skip that," I told him.

"Me, too," Maggie said.

I asked her, "How'd you know about Thief?"

"Nate told me."

Romeo said, "Most of the guys know. He's going to be our camp mascot. We were going to tell you, but we wanted to get him good and tame, first. 'Cause if there was an accident—I mean, he *is* a skunk—we didn't want any way that the captain could blame it on you."

I almost said, *You don't need to look out for me.* But I held it in. He hadn't meant harm.

I just said, "So Cold Day Camp has got a skunk named Thief for a mascot."

Maggie raised her eyebrows at Romeo, who looked like a kid caught red-handed at mischief.

"Actually," he said. "We've got two mascots."

He whistled, and a patch-eyed hound dog, all swayback and bones, slinked out.

"This here's Beggar," Romeo said. "He followed Thief here the other day, and I figured if he was hungry enough not to be scared of a skunk, he must need a handout pretty bad."

"Do the other fellows know about him, too?" I asked.

Romeo nodded. "We were going to tell you, honest."

"And who was going to tell the captain?"

"Oh, Sam's got a plan for that."

Sam's plan consisted of a photograph that ran on the front page of the *Monroe Herald*. The story that surrounded it talked about the reservoir and conservation program. But the caption under the photograph said, "Meet Beggar and Thief, the unlikely mascots of Company 597. It's a tribute to the CCC boys' spirits and to their commanding officer, Captain Hakes, that the Cold Day Camp is such a friendly place even a skunk and a pooch can get along there."

"Sam," I said, after reading it through twice, "you're not called the Senator for nothing. There's politicians in the Austin statehouse, down home, who've got nothing on you."

"I don't know about that," he said. "It seems to me you're the smart one, knowing how to make people get along and do what they should. And the fellows give you credit for it, even if the captain doesn't."

Chapter 29

Even before the open house, we'd already started working outside.

The fellows who'd be operating the camp's heavy equipment had begun learning how to do that. There'd been quite a competition for those slots, and I'd drawn names for the five allocated to my barracks.

I never heard how Compton decided on A Barracks' five operator jobs, but I doubted it was anything so simple.

Pops had a crew learning how to be surveyors as they staked in the boundaries of the reservoir and of a big chunk of prairie that was to be restored around it.

Another LEM was taking fellows down to the river, a few miles past where it ran by town, to cut willow starts. They'd be planted as soon as the ground would allow—a willow branch will root all by itself.

Apple was on the willow-cutting crew, and I asked him how it was going.

"Not bad work," he said, "except Compton seems to think he's in charge instead of the LEM who really is. You sure you don't want to invite him to be part of your shovel brigade?"

"Sure as certain," I answered. "Much as I would love to see him flinging mud."

By early April, the rest of us were working in mud all day long.

One of the first things we had to do was temporarily divert the creek, which was swelling with snowmelt from the mountains, far away as they were. The creek ran right through where our reservoir was going.

We made the diversion by digging a long channel around the land's shallow basin, starting up above it and rejoining the creek down below. Once we got that done, we stacked sandbags to wall off the natural streambed.

The army had loaned us a second bulldozer to go with the one we already had, and soon both were going nonstop. One towed a scraper across the bottom of the basin, removing layers of soil into the scraper body to be carried near where the dam and one bank were being built up. The second dozer, equipped with a plow blade, pushed the soil—mud mostly—closer.

But then it was muscle work. Dozens of us were kept as busy as agitated ants, shoveling the mud into wheelbarrows and running it up on top of the berms for other fellows to spread out.

And besides that, we had the spillway to build, and that meant preparing a base, laying in supports, and building forms before we could even begin pouring concrete. We wanted to have everything ready when the cement that was being ordered in from someplace arrived.

It was a lot going on, and it looked bad.

I was standing atop the berm one afternoon, resting on my shovel, when Nate came over.

"I know this mess is going to go away," he said. "But I hadn't pictured it."

"Me neither," I said. Every direction I looked, there was chewed-up earth spiky with ripped-out plant roots. No order at all till the Lundgren place, where a field was being prepared for planting.

"I wasn't sure Dad would go through with the changes," Nate said. "Back when it was just plan and pretend, they seemed like a great idea. But now, seeing him do things differently than he ever has—I'm sure hoping they're not going to prove a mistake."

"I don't see that they can," I said.

"He's putting less acreage into money crops. Even with the subsidy, they're going to have to come in good to balance out."

From where we were, we had a bird's-eye view of the work going on in the Lundgrens' nearest field. A tractor was plowing it into gently curving strips that hugged the roll of the land.

A horse team followed, dragging a wide, spike-toothed harrow, breaking up clumps of earth and leaving a pattern of stripes. "Who's driving the horses?" I asked Nate.

"Maggie," he said. "Even if I was home to do it, she'd be wanting to. She's a worker."

"Like us," a nearby fellow said. "Just prettier."

"No joke," someone answered, with enough edge to say he didn't think the way the 597th was working was any joke at all.

All the fellows were angry over how Captain Hakes was pushing us. Our eight-hour days had gone to ten and then twelve, and he'd worked us straight through two Saturdays.

And things were going to get worse, too, because we were about to lose twenty men to a spike camp Pops was to set up in the woods some distance away. We'd soon be needing the fence posts they were going after, but their departure would leave us down twenty workers.

"I don't get it," I said to Pops. "Why do we have to be in such a hurry?"

"I imagine the captain's concerned we get the reservoir filled before the snowmelt's all gone and the dry season hits," Pops said. "And the sooner we plant the willow starts and other trees, the longer growing season they'll have to take hold."

But Sam told me Hakes didn't know a growing season from a month of Sundays. What had Hakes stirred up was that district would be sending out an inspection team in a few weeks. "I keep telling you," Sam said. "With him it's all show."

"I don't care what his reason is. He's got everybody steamed," I said. "If he doesn't let up soon, I don't think I can keep a lid on."

Finally it got bad enough I decided that I had to at least try to do something.

At Compton's and my briefing meeting with Captain Hakes on a Tuesday toward the middle of the month, I said, "Sir, the fellows in my barracks could really use a break. It's not right to ask them to keep going so hard."

"According to whom?" Hakes said.

"Well, to me, I guess. I think—"

Compton cut me off. "I don't see a problem. The men in A Barracks aren't complaining."

That was a flat-out lie, but the captain didn't call him on it. "Of course they're not," he said. "Men's attitudes reflect the attitude of their leaders."

I tried again. "Sir, I don't think that when Mr. Caldwell laid out the project he intended for us to—"

"You will leave coordination with Mr. Caldwell to me," Hakes said. "Just worry about doing your own job, which is to make sure your men do theirs. Or is that asking too much?"

Then Captain Hakes did a sudden about-face.

Coming back from the field two days later, I stopped

by headquarters office to see if Sam was ready to knock off. He motioned me to be quiet and listen.

The captain's door was open, and Hakes and Pops were talking, neither one trying to keep their voices down.

Pops was saying our work schedule needed to ease up. "Pretty soon the boys are going to be talking mutiny," he said.

Hakes said, "They wouldn't dare."

"And working them so hard is against regulations," Pops went on. "The CCC specifies forty-hour work-weeks for these boys."

"Generally," Hakes said. "Circumstances can justify asking more."

"What you're doing is way beyond that."

"It is not."

A silence followed that Pops broke. He said, "Then I guess we must have a different understanding of the regulations. Why don't we just ask district headquarters for a clarification? Maybe I can do that before I leave for the spike camp tomorrow morning."

The next morning, Friday, we got ordered back to five-day workweeks, plus we were promised use of the stake trucks Saturday afternoon to take anybody into town who wanted to go.

We put in the best working day we had since the push started, with everybody in high spirits. And back in camp later on, I again swung by to see Sam.

"Captain Hakes should come out to the site and see for himself how hard everybody works when they're being treated fair," I said.

"I doubt he's going to do that," Sam said. "He's got a new worry on his mind now."

"What's that?"

"Some kind of paperwork muddle he needs to straighten out before the inspection team comes next month. He's spent the day matching up purchase and inventory records. Which reminds me. I've got some papers to take over to the mess sergeant. Come with me, and we'll see if Romeo can round us up some coffee."

Supper preparation was in full swing, the mess hall crew all in their cooks' whites, which they wore instead of denims. Steam curled above soup kettles, and tuna sandwiches were being turned out on an assembly line that Henry Ford himself would have approved of.

We found Romeo out back spoiling Beggar and Thief.

"Had to take me a break," he said. "I've been going since dawn when I had to make the run into town for perishables."

He glanced sideways at me, like he thought I might jack him up for slacking off.

I just shook my head. Getting Hakes to return the outside crew to forty-hour weeks was one thing. Getting him to stop piling double duty on everybody he could was another. Romeo hadn't ought to be expected to pick up supplies and then spend a whole day cooking them, both.

"That a whole egg you just gave Thief?" I asked.

"It had a crack in it," Romeo said.

Thief tapped a little hole in one end and commenced sucking the insides out. "I taught him that," Romeo said proudly.

"I thought it was hounds that're supposed to suck eggs," I said. "Though I never saw one."

"Me neither, and Beggar doesn't have the knack."

Beggar was sitting back on his haunches, watching the skunk with as much interest as us humans were.

Sam had on the expression I thought of as his Boston look, though I didn't know beans about Boston. But it was a look like just when he'd thought he'd seen everything, here came something new under the sun.

"Well," Sam said, "that explains part of the captain's problem, anyway."

"What's that?" Romeo asked.

"The mess sergeant complained that we're not ordering enough eggs, and I brought over the last purchase order to show him we're buying the same supplies as always: one hundred twenty dozen eggs per week, along with a half ton of bread and a quarter ton of beef. But of course, nobody figured on Thief's consumption."

Romeo appeared puzzled for a moment, like he was trying to work something out. But then Thief finished the egg and waddled back a few steps to watch for what might come next.

"No more," Romeo told him. "Sam," he said, "honest, Thief hasn't eaten...well, I've not exactly counted, but not enough eggs they'd be missed."

"Oh, I know that," Sam said. "We're talking dozens." He got to his feet. "Well, good coffee, but I came over to see the mess sergeant, so I better go find him. You going into town tomorrow?"

"Wouldn't miss it," Romeo said happily. "I'm going to buy some hooks and line for a fishing pole I made and try my luck on the river."

Chapter 30

Saturday afternoon we hit town in a celebrating mood.

Fellows scattered fast, one big group heading to the pool hall and another to the ice-cream parlor. Sam led a contingent to the library. Romeo went to buy his fishing tackle.

"Want to go to my place?" Nate asked me. "Maggie ought to be getting off work about now, and we could ride out with her since she probably drove the truck in."

"Sure," I said. I'd been hoping he'd ask.

But then I noticed, right across the street, the Rialto Cinema, and a line of people buying tickets for a matinee showing of *The Whole Town's Talking*. "Unless," I began, "maybe Maggie would like to go with us to…"

Nate said, "Not my kind of show. But if you two want to go, I don't mind. I'll spend the afternoon with my folks and then get the truck back to her."

Maggie didn't have to be asked twice. "I'd love to," she told me, without seeming to mind one bit that Nate wasn't going with us.

Maggie liked the cartoons as much as I did. She got impatient at a newsreel that showed a family going for a Sunday drive in a new car—"You tell me how many families you know with new cars!" she whispered. And she sighed with pleasure when the main feature, with Jean Arthur and Edward G. Robinson, started.

"I just love a good story, don't you?" she whispered.

Afterward, we went down to Mrs. Jensen's café for slices of pie. Though when I opened the door and the smell of good chili hit my nose, I revised my order. Truth to tell, it made me a bit homesick for Texas.

And if the chili—just meat and no beans—wasn't enough to say where Pops's wife was from, the photographs covering the wall were. They mostly showed people posed in front of landmarks like the Alamo. Mrs. Jensen saw me looking and came over to point out one of a pretty girl in an old-fashioned outfit.

"Me, the day I became a Harvey Girl," she said. "You know about those?"

I shook my head.

"We waitressed in restaurants all along the railroad lines, living in dormitories. We worked hard and got to see some of the world. That's how I met Lester."

It took me a second to realize she meant Pops.

"Though," she said, "if you'd told me serving coffee

to a stranger would lead to my living my life out here in Montana..." She shook her head. "Not that staying hasn't turned out good, mind you."

Then another customer came in.

Maggie gazed after Mrs. Jensen a moment and then turned to me. "How about you, Moss?" she asked, just loud enough for me to hear her over the radio Mrs. Jensen had playing. "Are you thinking about staying up here?"

The question caught me by surprise, and I blurted out, "Oh no. This is just temporary, until—"

I caught myself. *Until what?* With a start, I realized it had been some time since I'd thought about leaving. The good smell of chili reminding me of Muddy Springs notwithstanding.

"At least I guess it's temporary," I finished. "Though I got to say, I'm liking this country a lot, especially now it's warming up."

"You think you'll go back to farming?" she asked.

"I wasn't—" I began, and then once more I broke off. I was going to say I wasn't ever a farmer, but that wasn't wholly true. I grew up farming, even if my stint at the airport did do me a turn into other work.

I said, "I'm not planning to, though it's kind of hard to see much into the future."

Mrs. Jensen, turning up the radio volume, called, "Listen. This is about you."

It was Mr. Fechner, the director of the whole CCC, reading a message President Roosevelt had sent CCC'ers about all we'd accomplished so far. "'You and the men who have guided and supervised your efforts have cause to be proud…'"

"He's right," Maggie said, when the broadcast ended. "The country is turning around, and the CCC's helping it to. Just like our place is going to turn around, with all the changes Dad's making. There's a future there."

"Well, sure," I said.

"For someone who wants to farm it," she said. "But I don't think Nate does."

"No," I agreed.

Maggie examined her piecrust like it was the most interesting thing she'd seen all day, and then she suddenly said, "Nate said you had a girlfriend down in Texas. With an unusual name."

"Beatty," I responded.

"What's she think?"

"About what?" I asked cautiously. I wasn't sure where Maggie was heading, but I doubted I was going to like getting there.

"Well, about you seeing me."

"I don't know," I answered. "She doesn't—"

"Moss," Maggie said, her voice sharpening. "You are being honest with Beatty and me, aren't you?"

"Well," I said again, grasping for something that wouldn't make me sound too bad. "I haven't exactly written her…"

"About me?" Maggie asked. Then a look of disbelief crossed her face. "Or haven't you written her at all?"

"I'm working up to it," I said, but Maggie didn't buy that for an instant.

"Well, when you *finish* working up to it," she said, "let me know." She put fifteen cents on the table. "I enjoyed the pie, Mrs. Jensen."

"Wait," I said. "I'm treating to that."

But Maggie was across the floor and out the door like I hadn't spoken.

If my afternoon in town ended less than great, I seemed to be the only one wishing for things to have been different.

The pool hall crowd spent the truck ride back recounting, shot by shot, their games of snooker. A couple of guys were pleased about town girls they'd met. Sam clutched a stack of library books. And Romeo had a corner of the truck to himself, because of the string of rainbow trout he was taking to Beggar and Thief.

I felt downright warmhearted toward them all. Straightforward, they were. Good fellows who didn't throw you a curve when you weren't expecting one. I hadn't noticed any of them worrying if I'd caught up on my letter writing.

Maggie could take a lesson.

Beatty, too, for all I knew.

Chapter 31

I got back to camp to find another letter from Beatty waiting for me. She still didn't seem angry I hadn't written. Just, maybe, on the sharp side of perplexed.

But her letter brought a complication. Annie Boudreau, the woman pilot who had her own flying business and had taught Beatty to fly, was planning a trip to the new airport just outside Yellowstone Park. *Annie's thinking about flying tourist groups up and wants to see the facilities,* Beatty wrote.

I've got permission to take a Friday off from school so I can go up with her. We'll get in around dinnertime May 1 and leave the following afternoon. I've been studying a map, and it looks like Monroe's less than two hundred miles away. I know that's not real close, but it's not a hopeless distance, either. Could you possibly come down? I'd so much like to see you.

My heart kind of bounced a bit at the idea of it. She *still* wanted to see me.

But there wasn't a chance in the world Hakes would give me a weekend pass.

No point in even asking.

There was just too much going on at work as we raced the season.

And the project was turning around. Where things had been looking more torn up with each day, now they started taking on the shape of how they'd be.

It sorrowed me Pops wasn't around to see the first of the willow starts go in the ground. Not that they looked particularly promising.

But then at lunchtime just a couple of days later, when everybody was sitting around eating our baked-bean sandwiches, Apple suddenly exclaimed, "Would you look yonder!"

And there, flitting from one willow whip to the next was a red-winged blackbird, looking for all the world like he was on an inspection trip.

"Think he wants to homestead?" Sam said.

"Probably got a missus someplace who told him just what kind of nesting spot she wants," a LEM named Scotty answered. A nice guy, though of course he wasn't Pops. "Could be they'll be our first residents."

With Pops off to the spike camp, Scotty had taken over being foreman on the spillway work. We'd been pouring concrete in lifts over several days, but when we did our first batch for Scotty, he gave us the same lecture Pops had.

"Concrete," he said, "is the result of a chemical reaction that happens when cement, water, sand, and gravel are mixed together. Get the proportions right and you will get a dam that will outlast anybody here. Get them wrong and you'll have weakness."

"How would we know?" someone asked.

"You can tell bad concrete by the color or by holes in it," he said. "But you're not going to be seeing any signs of weakness here because there won't be any. Like Pops must have told you, you're to be as careful measuring as if you were following your mamas' recipes."

The whole company gathered to watch the forms come off, and when I saw we had us a spillway smooth as a baby's bottom, I couldn't have been more proud.

It was plain gorgeous, six feet long and flanked on either side by the earthen berm. An honest twelve feet thick at the bottom, and tapering up on the spillover side. The top, instead of being straight across, was notched in the middle to take the control gate we'd be setting in it.

Scotty said, "Looks like a winner. It's curing a mite different than I've seen concrete cure before, but there's not an air pocket to be seen, or a band of unmixed material. Good work, men."

Sam pulled out the camp camera—besides all Sam's other jobs, Captain Hakes had recently assigned him to gather material for the camp yearbook that district wanted done. "Everybody," he said, "group together so I can get a photo. Out on the berm."

He took forever posing us, because of how hard it was to get a shot that didn't have somebody in the way of somebody else. Or a guy making devil's horns over another fellow's head.

It gave me time to look around and be satisfied. And to notice, too, that over at the Lundgren place, the tractor was now pulling a seed drill.

We let the concrete set up one more day, for good measure, and then the whole company again gathered. This time we were celebrating removing the sandbags that had kept water from running through the reservoir while we were digging it.

With its old bed no longer intact, the creek seemed to feel its way at first, running in spurts down mud paths and tractor tracks. And then like a horse that smelled home, the water began moving faster into the bottom of the basin. It spread out there, slowed by the mud, but eventually a stream made its way to the far end, where it was stopped by our dam.

We watched and watched, till glistening pools of water pocked the whole basin bottom and crept up the concrete of the spillway.

Our reservoir was filling.

I didn't know who started yelling. Somebody. And then we all picked it up.

Maggie said later her mother flew out the house, scared that something was wrong.

But it was just us. The 597th crowing to the world what we'd done.

Everything was moving right fast that last part of April. A yellow green haze had settled over the land almost overnight, and now the earth was taking on all the shades of early leaves and new grass.

The Montanans called it *green up,* as if it was a season of its own. They said *green up* in throwaway tones like they were hoping to hide how they felt, but their eyes gave away how they welcomed it.

We pitched ourselves into helping it along. We planted the rest of the willows, along with all kinds of baby trees a CCC nursery sent us. On the prairie land marked for restoring, we seeded native grasses. We rechanneled gullies to direct runoff into the reservoir instead of onto the county road.

There were setbacks, sure: A batch of poplar saplings died without ever leafing out. One of the stake trucks went out of control going down a hill and crashed hard enough to cause damage, though luckily nobody got hurt. A flash thunderstorm washed out a bunch of shrubs, reminding us all how vulnerable soil was when it didn't have a good network of roots holding it.

And as April ended, off and on wet, rainy weather kept things off and on muddy.

But the setbacks were far outweighed by the progress we could see all around us. At the rate the reservoir was filling, water would soon be going over the spillway, running down the old creek bed and on through the Lundgren place again. Over there, the first of the seeded fields was coming up, the curving strips of tiny wheat sprouts a darker color than the younger barley next to them.

And each day brought surprises. A mate for that red-winged blackbird Apple had spotted, along with a passel of their relatives.

A killdeer putting on a show of having a broken wing, to divert the attention of anyone about to discover her ground nest.

A mule deer atop the berm one morning.

A red fox running off.

Wildflowers.

Chapter 32

No two ways about it, the end of April was a grand time, only marred by knowing that for some of us, it would end soon.

We'd signed on for six-month hitches, and they'd be up before the middle of May. A fellow couldn't go anywhere without hearing somebody agonizing over whether to sign on for a second six months.

Nate made his decision early. "I'm going to work with Dad through harvest, anyway," he said. "Probably I'll be back for another winter term in the CCC, but maybe not. Maybe the crops will come in good enough he'll at least *talk* about college with me."

Riley Maxwell went back and forth with a couple of other southerners before all three decided that since they'd lived through a Montana winter, they deserved some summer under the Big Sky.

Apple just quietly said, "I'm in for another round."

Only Sam was silent on the subject. For a while I

thought it was because he was too busy putting together the camp yearbook to think of much else. Sam had taught Hal Linchfeld to use the camera, but he had saved the writing for himself. He said he was going to include highlights of all that had gone on during our hitches, both in camp and out, and he was still working on that.

"It's a yearbook," I told him. "You don't have to turn it into the *Iliad*." By then, Mr. Romsteder had our Great Works class reading Homer.

"I'm not trying to," Sam said. He had a pile of newspaper clippings spread out on his bed. There was a headline about how a dirigible, the *Hindenburg,* was scheduling a flight across the Atlantic Ocean. "But you remember how Apple got us all putting our initials on the entrance?"

"Yeah. Sure."

"I want to place us, too. And not only with a record that we were in the Cold Day Camp in 1936, but that we were here in the *world* now, too. In case we ever might need remembering how it was."

"Sam," I said, "even for you, that's a pretty mixed-up thing to say. And you really don't need to work so hard."

"I don't mind," he said. Then, looking away, he added, "Anyway, I owe the 597th a lot. This is my thank-you."

It hit hard. "That's your way of saying you're getting out?"

He nodded. "This came today." He handed over a typed letter of acceptance from the University of Michigan.

"I didn't know you'd applied," I said.

"You told me to rethink what I'd said about not going back to school. Deep down I knew I needed to. And then you gave me that shove."

"Yeah," I said, "but I didn't mean for you to do it all right now." *First Nate saying he'd be leaving. Now Sam. And it was my own fault that Sam was going.*

"They're giving me a small scholarship," he said. "Mr. Romsteder thinks I can get a job waiting tables and washing dishes at a fraternity house, and I'm hoping to find a rooming house where I can stay in exchange for doing chores."

"That's great," I told him. "Sounds like you've got it all worked out. And your folks ought to be pleased."

"I suppose," he said. "Though that's not the reason I'm doing it. Just the opposite. I'm still mad enough at them, I'd like to stay out of school forever to get back. But Mr. Romsteder's helped me see that I'd just be hurting myself."

"Cutting your nose off to spite your face," I said. "I guess you would be."

Sam wasn't the only one who'd gotten news in the mail.

I pulled out a letter from Ma that I'd already read more than once.

Dear Moss, she'd written. *I wished you might see*

how good things are here and you are a lot the reason. I know as you meant me to use your CCC pay money for the little ones and I have been, but with some of your extra leader pay I bought myself a dress and shoes not to be ashamed of.

Then I said to Mr. Willis at the Dry Goods didn't he need somebody selling yard goods who can find the straight of the material. Goodness knows he has been making ladies unhappy with his cuts that make you throw so much in the scrap bag before you can lay out a pattern. He said he would try me in Fabrics and Notions, and business has picked up there so I am now on regular.

Also your Pa is now appered on the earth again, and is on the WPA, only in Calif. this time, so between all I breethe easier than in years. Not forgetting you pitched in when I was so worried how even to buy food. You are a good boy, Moss.

Yr loving mother, Bertha Trawnley.

I put the letter back in its envelope.

I'd forgotten how my ma could go on a mile a minute, breathless and happy, telling all the parts of a tale at once. I was probably the only one of us kids who even remembered her that way. But it was how she used to talk, before.

So, Ma was finally facing down the Depression.

I wouldn't give a plugged nickel for the chances Pa would stay on the WPA job, but she'd found a way to support herself and the kids. And I'd helped her.

It gave me a start to realize I'd done what I'd left Texas to do—I'd tracked down Pa, taken care of myself, and given my family a hand—and now my family didn't need me so much. Probably I could go out on my own if I wanted to.

Only now that it was a choice, I didn't think that's what I wanted.

And it wasn't just not having something else to do that held me. Despite having to work with Compton and for Hakes, I'd enjoyed being in the CCC.

And I was proud of what the 597th had got done. We'd turned a piece of worn-out land into something good, and we'd helped farmers like Mr. Lundgren find new ways to farm.

Part of me wanted to leave before something bad could come along to spoil things, but part of me wanted to stay around to see the job a little further along.

Anyway, I was finally ready to write to Beatty. I had something proud to tell her, even though it probably wasn't exactly what she wanted to hear.

It's Thursday, I thought. *Maybe if I put an airmail stamp on the envelope and mail it today, she'll get it Monday, right after returning from her trip to Yellowstone.*

I got my writing stuff and began. *Dear Beatty, First, I am sorry I put this off so long. And I am sorry how I left Muddy Springs without*

Apple interrupted me.

"Moss," he said, "you got a minute to go over to the garage with me? There's something I need to show you."

He showed me a tie-rod, which was a piece kind of like a metal broom handle that kept a vehicle's wheels going in the same direction.

"What about it?" I asked.

"Look there," he said, tapping it with his finger. I squinted and finally saw a hairline crack, tiny enough to be almost invisible.

"Is this from the wrecked truck?" I asked.

"That's just it. It's not," Apple answered. "The one we took out of the truck was broken clear through, in the same place. We figured it broke in the accident, which was a shame, because we'd put it in new just the month before.

"But then this afternoon I was over here pulling out some spare parts for the engine repairs class, and the beam from my flashlight caught this. Without the flashlight I wouldn't have spotted it, and I doubt anyone installing it would, either."

He said, "Moss, you know a lot about mechanics. If the truck's tie-rod failed, couldn't that have caused the truck to go out of control?"

"Yes, of course," I said. "A broken tie-rod would make the steering go haywire."

Then, with a sinking feeling, I realized what he was getting at. I told myself it had to be a coincidence. The last thing I wanted right then was another problem.

But I said, "Apple, what do *you* think the chances are that two parts, one of them new, would have exactly the same fault?"

"Actually," he said. "We got in three tie-rods at the same time. Those two and then one we put in a truck that we returned to the Forest Service back when its season geared up. The truck hadn't needed it, but we made the replacement for practice."

I studied the piece I was holding. Already I'd lost sight of the tiny crack in it. "Do you know where we get our spare parts?"

He shook his head. "Army supply, maybe? Sam might know. He does paperwork."

"Depends on the part," Sam told me. "The army sends a lot of stuff—filters, gaskets, lightbulbs—whatever we need for regular maintenance. But other things we get from town."

"From the filling station?" I asked.

"Yes," he said. "Indirectly, anyway. Captain Hakes usually goes through Owen Schieling, because he can get us a better price."

Chapter 33

I wrestled with the problem all night. Captain Hakes had to be told.

But I hated the trouble I'd be causing Mr. Schieling, when he'd never been anything but supportive of the camp.

And I guess I dreaded facing the CO.

I couldn't see a way around it, though. Apple had brought the problem to me, trusting I'd know what to do. And so on getting up Friday morning, I asked Sam, "Do you think you can get me in to see the captain first thing?"

He pulled on his T-shirt. "I won't see him myself," he answered. "Sergeant Ruffino and I are driving into town right after breakfast to do errands. But you can probably just knock on his door."

"What?" Captain Hakes's voice, coming immediately on my knock, startled me. He opened the door so fast he must have been right at it. "Oh! Trawnley!" he said. He frowned. "Why aren't you at the work site?"

"There's something I need to talk to you about, sir. It's important."

"It had better be," he said.

I explained about the cracked and broken tie-rods.

"So?" he said. "Tell Enrollee Durgan to give the faulty spare to Sergeant Ruffino. He'll see that it gets exchanged."

"I will, sir," I said. "But Apple—Enrollee Durgan— told me the class also replaced a tie-rod on a truck we had to give back to the Forest Service. So you need to warn them, or to ask district to, in case that one was bad, too."

A pulse started throbbing on the side of the captain's neck. "Are you trying to tell me how to do my job?"

"No, sir," I said, knowing I'd better shut up. But I wasn't certain he intended to pass along the warning, and if there was another accident, maybe this time somebody would get hurt. I said, "But you *are* going to do something?"

Captain Hakes exploded.

"Yes!" he said. "I'm going to do something about your negative attitude and your idea that you're running this camp instead of me. As of this minute, you are again Enrollee Trawnley. You can leave your armband on Sergeant Ruffino's desk."

It was the last thing I'd expected, and my knees

actually almost buckled under me. I was losing my job? For trying to do it?

"I've had enough of you, Trawnley," he said. "Now take off, and keep your mouth shut!" His eyes locked on mine. "Because if I hear any rumors being spread about bad vehicle parts or anything else, you will find yourself not only out of your leader's pay. You'll be out of the CCC.

"And Trawnley," he added, "when you get to the job site, tell Junior Leader Compton I want to see him. I'll have him help run both barracks until I select your replacement."

The room seemed to be shimmying around me, and my breath felt like it was stuck.

He couldn't just expect me to go out to the reservoir, where someone would be sure to tell me I'd forgotten my armband. And then somebody else would see Compton gloat, when I gave him the message. And word would go around...

"What are you waiting for, Trawnley?" Hakes asked, reaching for his desk calendar. He flipped a page, to May.

It was May 1. There was an answer. Or at least a way to put things off.

"Sir," I said, "I know you're not giving weekend passes right now, but if you would please..."

"No, you're not getting a pass! Do you think I'm going to reward—" He broke off as though he'd just thought of something. "Perhaps you're right," he said.

"Perhaps the transition will go easier if you're gone for a couple of days."

He got out a form and rapidly filled in the blanks. "Here," he said. "This starts now. Be back Sunday night."

Somehow my legs got me outside, but just barely. I leaned against the building wall for the longest time, waiting for the rubbery feeling to go out of them. Waiting for my heart to stop racing and for the roaring in my head to go away. The noise was so loud I missed the first part of a phone call going on inside, near the window right over my head.

"I don't want to hear why," Captain Hakes was saying. "Just get out here and exchange it. I've looked the other way for the last time, Schieling. Low-grade coal, spoiled meat, late supplies, bad counts—I could balance some of that against what you saved the camp's budget. But endangering lives..."

I was more disgusted than I'd ever been with anything in my life.

Here the guys had been working their hearts out on their CCC jobs, while all along they were being short-changed by a camp commander out to skimp at their expense. And not for the good of the camp, that was for sure, but for how it would look good on Hakes's record.

I guessed I shouldn't have been surprised at Hakes. He'd never given reason to expect more.

But Mr. Schieling...I'd liked him. I'd *trusted* him.

I kicked a rock hard as I could. The Depression. The endless, blasted, *blasted* Depression. All it did was make people be less than you expected, until it took them away from you altogether.

I was so mad I barely registered Mr. Caldwell's driving up and going inside. But I did hear what he said.

"I don't want to raise a false alarm," he told Hakes. "But I was just up at the project site, inspecting the spillway. It looks good enough, but if you hit an edge with a hammer, concrete chips off. It shouldn't do that."

"It's probably still curing," Hakes said.

"No. That's not how concrete cures. Either the mixing proportions were off or, just possibly, the cement we used was bad. I just hope it's only the top lift that's a problem. We can patch that."

I was lucky with the trains, and able to ride boxcars pretty much one right after another as far as Bozeman. Then a guy driving an empty logging truck took me the rest of the way, a dreary drive through rain that lasted until we were almost to the park.

I didn't get into the town of West Yellowstone until after dark, but I didn't have any trouble finding Beatty. She and Annie Boudreau had set up a tent on the airport grounds and were finishing up a supper they'd cooked over a small fire.

As fast as the firelight flickered, expressions chased

across Beatty's face when she saw me. And then she scrambled up.

"Moss!" she said, hugging me. "I was hoping so much...I've missed you so much, and I've been so worried about you. And then I was afraid you wouldn't get my telegram in time to get down here. But you must have."

"I got your letter," I said, "not a telegram."

Annie clanked some dishes, and I turned, late with my manners.

She gave me a hug, too, but then said, "Don't you two mind me. I'm just going to slip over to the operations room to see what the weather's looking like for tomorrow."

I told Beatty, "I'm sorry you went to the cost of telegraphing. I should have answered the letter you sent about coming up here."

"But that wasn't why we wired you," she said. "It was to tell you the airport's holding your old job for you. You do want it, don't you?"

"Well, yeah, of course. Beatty, I don't understand. What happened to the man who replaced me?"

"Mr. Kliber's cousin? He should never have been hired. He thought he was too good to do things like cleaning, got high-handed with customers, wouldn't take instructions from anybody. Then he misplaced a mail pouch, and all the trouble that caused was the last straw. He quit about one second ahead of being fired."

I was only half taking in the details. The rest of my mind was thinking how this solved everything. I had something to do when my hitch was up. And facing the fellows back at camp wouldn't be so bad. Now I could tell them, Yeah, I'd lost my junior leader job, but I had a real job waiting.

"So you'll come back to Muddy Springs?" Beatty asked.

"My hitch is up in another ten days," I answered. "Right after that."

"The airport board won't hold it open that long," Beatty said. "That's why we telegraphed you. We want you to go back with us."

"Well, I guess I could go," I said, thinking aloud. "I'm close enough to getting out anyway, and probably my CO would just as soon have me gone. I doubt he'd try to get me back.

"There's some guys I'd like to say good-bye to, but I guess I can write them."

Beatty said, "Maybe you can do that tomorrow. First, now that the airport job's settled, you've got some catching up to do." She slid me a look. "And some explaining, maybe? Why you never did write? I worried, just a little, you might have found a girl up in Montana."

I was saved from having to answer by Annie's return. "The forecast isn't good," she said. "Occasional rain through the night, getting heavier through the weekend, with increasing likelihood of thunderstorms.

I think we better wrap our business up here as quickly as possible in the morning and then head out."

She turned to me. "Are you going with us, Moss?"

"Well, if there's room."

"Sure. We flew up a four-seater, and Beatty and I just make two." Annie made a production of yawning. "I think I'll turn in."

Beatty and I talked and talked. She told me everything I'd missed in Muddy Springs. I told her all about being in the CCC, and about the fellows, and about 597th's projects. I even told her about Maggie. Some, anyhow. "She's a really nice girl."

"Would she have become your girl if you'd stayed in Montana?" Beatty asked.

"No. It's not like with us. She and I want different things. She was already figuring that out."

It wasn't till I'd finally wound down that Beatty said, "What you haven't told me is what took you to Montana to start with. I could understand your leaving Muddy Springs, but why did you go all the way up there?"

So then I started back at the beginning, with that first letter from Ma. Beatty was the one person in the world I'd never tried to hide anything from, and I wasn't starting now.

It felt good to finally tell it all.

She just held my hand. "I guess you felt pretty abandoned," she said. "Like I still do sometimes, when my dad gets so busy with his airline jobs he puts off visiting. Only that's nothing compared to, well..."

"I won't ever be like my pa," I told her. "When people count on me, I won't let them down."

Fast as I said those words, they hit me about as hard as anything ever had.

Because that was just what I was doing, wasn't it?

I was going off and leaving my fellows to Hakes and Compton. To whatever else might happen if Hakes didn't deal with the equipment problems. To disappointment over having to put patches on a project the fellows had thought was perfect.

I guessed they'd get over it, especially the ones who wouldn't be coming back for second hitches, but that didn't make it right. I didn't want it that way for any of them.

And I didn't want to be my pa.

Chapter 34

The trip back to Monroe took a day and most of a night, what with rain-slicked roads slowing traffic and storms sidelining one of the trains I hopped.

The station was locked, and so I started walking toward camp. The morning was damp and blowy, and every step landed me in another puddle, but at least it wasn't raining for the moment.

A dairy truck pulled up. "You one of the CCC'ers?" the driver asked. "I got rounds to do in the other direction first, but if you want to jump in, I'll get you to your camp by breakfast."

"Thanks," I said, getting in. "I can't believe how wet everything is. It was dry when I left here the day before yesterday."

"You just missed the start of one downpour after another then," he said. "The rain's been hard on folks who've got new crops in or young calves out on pasture. One of my regulars lost a panicky little heifer that drowned in a swollen creek."

I couldn't see much beyond the slick mud of the road in the truck's headlights. "You hear how any-body else is doing?" I asked. "The Lundgrens?"

"Hanging in there, I think," the driver replied. "I saw the one kid in town yesterday, getting sandbags."

"The kid? Maggie Lundgren?"

"No. Her brother, Nate."

"He must have got the weekend off then. Are you going by their place?" I asked.

"Yeah. You want me to drop you off?"

"If you would, I'd be obliged."

I'd hoped somebody would be up already, but the Lundgrens' was still dark when the truck left me at the drive. Not wanting to wake the whole family, I walked around back and knocked on the window of Nate's room off the kitchen.

"Hey, it's me. Moss," I called softly.

I heard Nate mutter and then repeat, "Moss?"

"Yeah."

"What are you...just a minute."

A moment later a kerosene lamp lit up in the kitchen, and then Nate let me in. If I'd expected a wel-come, I didn't get it. He looked exhausted and like he didn't want one more thing to deal with. "What are you doing here?" he asked.

"I thought maybe you could use some help. I'm on a pass till this evening. But, look, I'm sorry I woke you. If you want to go back to bed, I can stretch out in here for a couple of hours."

He fed some kindling into the stove and coaxed along glowing coals. "I need to be up," he said. "You want to put some water in the coffeepot while I do this?"

I worked the pump at the sink, letting the first, dirty jet of water go by and then catching the clean that followed. "The man who dropped me off said the weather's been causing problems. Are you all going to be okay?"

"I don't know," he said. "We're worried the wheat and barley will wash out."

"You don't think the contour rows will be enough to protect them?"

"From rain, maybe. Not from the gush of water we'll get if the reservoir dam breaks."

"Breaks! Why would it?"

"Because the spillway's failing. When the water level went way up Friday and yesterday, the concrete started breaking away in chunks. The floodgate's already torn out."

So it wasn't just the top lift that was bad, like Mr. Caldwell had hoped.

"Does anybody know why?" I asked.

"Scotty swears the mixing was all done right, and he vouches for the quality of the sand, gravel, and water. That just leaves faulty cement. It's got the guys really angry."

"I don't blame them," I said. "But what's being done to fix things?"

"Nothing," Nate said, his voice suddenly hard.

"What do you mean, nothing? Why not?"

"The guys are on strike," he said.

For a moment all I could do was stare. "But why?"

"Because of you, to start with," he said. "Compton didn't waste any time Friday letting everybody know you'd been demoted. I don't know what he expected...that it would be some kind of lesson, I guess.

"But it just made fellows mad. Everybody—even the guys in Compton's barracks—knew you'd worked your tail off on the reservoir. And, hell, you'd had a hand in just about everything *good* about the camp."

"But..."

"And then somebody said we ought to slow down work for the rest of Friday in protest. Guys were saying that's what organized labor does sometimes."

I said, "So guys aren't exactly on strike?"

"Oh yeah," Nate answered. "Getting angry about you was just the start of things. Compton made a lot of threats he couldn't carry out, and that got people even madder.

"And then yesterday, when word came in about the spillway starting to fail—along with the rumor it was because we'd been supplied with bad cement—Hakes pulled Saturday passes and ordered everybody to work shoring it up.

"That's when somebody said he'd built the dam once but he'd be danged if he was going to build it twice, and especially not on his weekend off."

That didn't sound at all like the guys I knew. "But Sam? Apple? What did they say?"

"I didn't wait to hear," Nate said. "That's when I left."

It was a lot to take in.

I asked Nate, "What are you going to do here?"

"The only things we can. Spread some straw, sandbag as best we can, and hope the worst of the rain's over. We need the reservoir to drop back some, not fill up more."

We both looked to the window, being hit by occasional drops.

I pulled on my jacket. "At least I can give you a hand with the straw. I'll go get started."

Mr. Lundgren spoke from the foot of the steps. "We'll get along without your help."

"But I'd like to..."

Turning his back to me, he said to Nate, "Tell him I don't want any more to do with the CCCs. If it wasn't for them, we wouldn't have a dam above our fields."

Nate didn't repeat it, of course, but he didn't say anything else, either, and after a moment I awkwardly took my leave.

I'd hardly got back on the road when Maggie came running after me. She was still wearing her nightclothes. A quilt she'd wrapped around herself flapped out.

"Moss, wait. I heard Dad. He was wrong to take his worry out on you, but he'll get over it." She glanced toward the house. "At least, if the crops don't get flooded out, he will."

A fine drizzle started up. "You want to go wait this out in the barn?" she asked.

"If I can't do anything here, then I ought to get to camp," I answered.

"Before you go...Are you going to tell me where you went?"

I looked down at her, realizing I'd likely never again see her face so close-up. I must have taken a shade too long to answer.

"It had to do with Beatty, didn't it?" she said.

I nodded.

She looked away. "I was guessing that. But it was pretty much over between us, anyway, wasn't it? Not that anything ever really started."

"Maggie, I wish—" I stopped, not sure what I did want.

"It's okay, Moss," she said. "It really, really is."

She pulled her quilt tighter. "I better go get some clothes on, so I can help Dad and Nate. And if you want to do something, you might try talking sense into that camp. It's got a responsibility that's not being met by a work strike."

"I'm going to try," I told her. "I am going to try."

Chapter 35

A woman driving a pickup with several crates of eggs in the back gave me a ride to town, and the Feed & Grain delivery driver, working despite its being Sunday, took me the rest of the way to the Cold Day Camp entrance. The grounds were deserted, and I angled over to the mess hall, figuring everyone was at breakfast.

But inside, there was only Sam, Sergeant Ruffino, and the kitchen crew drinking coffee. When they saw me, there were surprised exclamations from everybody but Sam. He just nodded. "Good to see you back," he said.

"Thought I'd try to help, if Captain Hakes will let me," I said.

"Hakes isn't letting anybody do anything," Romeo said. "He won't even let us make meals until the guys agree to go back to work. But I guess you don't know that the camp's on strike."

"Nate told me. I stopped by his place on my way here. But no meals? What's everybody eating?"

"We were just trying to figure that out," the mess sergeant said. "I was thinking we might put out bread and peanut butter for people to help themselves. I can't disobey orders, but I don't want to see the fellows go hungry, either."

"Are you going to fix things, Moss?" Romeo asked.

An A Barracks guy I didn't know very well laughed. "What makes you think the guys will listen to Trawnley? They wouldn't listen to President Roosevelt himself right now."

Sergeant Ruffino banged his hand on the table. "Will you get it in your head this isn't something to joke about? Lord knows what's going to happen to us military over this, but I can tell you what's going to happen to you kids. You're going to end up out on your ears, with no more jobs, no nothing."

"You really think that?" the kid asked, in a shocked voice.

I asked Sergeant Ruffino, "Won't they listen to you?"

"I don't know," he said. "The captain's ordered all the military staff to stay out of things and let them cook their own gooses. His words. To tell the truth, Moss, he's not making much sense."

That was shocker enough to halt conversation for a bit. Then I asked, "What's Compton doing?"

"Giving orders right and left. Only nobody's listening."

"I'll listen," I said. "If he's trying to get the fellows

to go to work, then I'm going to help him any way I can. And at least us here and Apple...Where is Apple?"

Sam said, "On strike."

Half the guys in B Barracks were still in their beds, and the other half were milling around arguing about whether they ought to storm the kitchen. That stopped when they saw me. I heard some "Hi's" and a "Hey! Look who's back!" There were some cheers, too, but I also caught some hostile glances.

Charlie Winden said, "If you're going to tell us to go to work, you can forget it."

"I'm not," I said. "I'm just looking for Bill Compton, to tell him some of us are going out to the project site to see what we can do."

"Compton's not here."

"I can see that," I said. "I'll go check the other barracks."

Cal slipped between me and the door. "I'm sorry, Moss," he said. "But you can't do that. You can't go to work."

"Sure I can," I said.

Others moved in, ringing us. Charlie said, "Strikes don't work unless everybody takes part. If you didn't want to be part of this one, you should have stayed away."

I tried pushing my way to the door, and someone grabbed my arm. Whirling around, I saw it was Apple who'd stopped me.

He said, "Charlie's right, Moss. The only way we're going to win is if we show them we're all in this together."

I stared at him—one of my best friends—not able to believe what I was hearing. "Win what? You aren't going to win anything except a bunch of discharges out of the CCC. Now let me by."

I shoved again but then turned back. "Look," I said, talking to everybody, "whatever your beef is—and I know you've got some real ones—it's not with Nate Lundgren. Are you going to let him and his folks get hurt, just so you can make a point?"

"If we've got to!" Apple answered fast.

We must have stared at each other a full half minute. I was wondering how I could have got him so wrong.

Then he nodded. "I'll go with you," he said.

Nobody tried to stop us after that, but no one else joined us, either. As we stepped out onto the sodden ground, Apple said, "You know we're not going to be able to do much by ourselves. Except maybe not have to feel quite so bad when the dam gives. If it does."

Then he waved toward the sky, dark and full of clouds, and said, "And it probably will."

A patter of raindrops was already signaling the start of a new downpour. I wondered how much rain would need to come down before the pressure of water in the reservoir became too much for the crumbling concrete work to withstand.

I could imagine how it would be: roiling, rain-swept water creeping higher and higher against the failing spillway, going into the cracks, wearing away at the weak points, pushing harder and harder, till suddenly...

Maybe a single spout of water would break through, but that would be enough. There'd be a roar as the water tore through the breached wall and poured out toward the Lundgrens' fields, with all those acres of fragile young plants.

Likely, too, the sudden rush of water would take some of the reservoir berm with it, along with willows and shrubs that hadn't had time to take root.

I wondered if the disaster would be enough to cause the Cold Day Camp to fold. Maybe nobody around Monroe would put trust in the camp again. Maybe they'd turn their backs on the good ideas our project was supposed to teach.

What did Apple say? Going out alone, we'd just be giving ourselves a reason not to feel so bad?

I told him, "You're right. We've got to take the others with us."

"Listen," I said in a voice so loud I didn't know who was most startled by it, B Barracks or me. But it got me a moment of quiet that I knew was all the chance I'd have to pick what I wanted to say.

"Apple was right, saying we've got to show them we're all in this together," I began.

"Most of us joined the CCC because we didn't have

any choice. The Depression got to be too much for us and our families to stand up to alone. Then we came here and saw how, by working together, we've got the power to change things. You want to give that up? And just to pay back a couple of people not worth our time?"

I had their attention.

"One more thing," I added. "Here, it's the Lundgrens' place at risk. But maybe near your homes there's other CCC camps trying to help your folks. You want those guys to give up when things don't go right?

"I don't know what it's going to take to save the reservoir and the Lundgrens' crops. But I think there's not much the 597th can't do, if we set our minds to it."

I looked around and then threw everything into one question, knowing it was the only roll of the dice I'd get. "I'm not your junior leader anymore. I can't tell you to do anything. But I can ask. Will you guys go with me?"

Charlie Winden walked over to his footlocker and pulled out work gloves, and Cal reached for his rain slicker.

Chapter 36

When A Barracks saw the whole of B Barracks running for the equipment sheds and garages, they came hurrying out, pulling on rain gear, calling questions. There was an excitement in the bustle and a hurrying purpose, like everyone was relieved to be back at work.

"Shovels," I said, calling out what we'd need as I thought of it. "Get shovels, picks, all the sandbags. Drivers, be sure you've got full tanks of gas."

Out of the corner of my eye I saw Compton hurrying toward me, blowing on a whistle. "What the hell are you doing back here?" he demanded. "And who told you to take over?"

"Nobody. They're your guys."

"Then see you remember it," he said. He raised his voice. "Okay," he yelled. "Listen up. I want..."

He ranted on, ignored by everybody. All by themselves, the guys got the equipment together, sorted themselves into the trucks, and got under way.

I jumped into the back of the last one. "Come on," I yelled at him.

He stayed put.

Scotty and Mr. Caldwell were already at the reservoir. They were standing up on the berm, wind blowing at them, the rain that had once again started up beating into their faces. I knew they were glad to see us, but they didn't waste words saying so.

"Just tell us how you want things shored up," I said.

Mr. Caldwell shook his head. "Shoring up's not going to work," he said. "There's nothing we can put up that will keep the water from breaking out if the spillway gives. But there may be another way, if we can do it in time. Scotty and I were just talking."

He knelt down in the mud and drew a rough picture of the reservoir and the area around it. "Our immediate problem is reducing the pressure against the spillway."

He scratched in a long line, from above the higher end of the reservoir banks all the way around the one on the far left side. "Here's that channel where we had the creek diverted through before. We can open it up again and stop the creek from adding to the reservoir."

Then he marked a spot on one side of the reservoir, down toward the lower end of the bank we'd built up to give some height to the land's natural basin. "And if we dig through the bank here, that will let a lot of water out."

I looked from his drawing to the Lundgren fields. "What's going to happen out there?" I asked. "Will the channel and creek bed be able to catch all the water and keep it contained?"

"No," Mr. Caldwell said. "It's going to come out in a rush way too fast."

"We brought sandbags," I said. "Can we do something with those?"

It was Scotty who suggested using them to build a long, low wall between the reservoir and the Lundgren place.

Mr. Caldwell nodded. "The sandbags won't stop the water, but they may slow it way down."

A sudden sweep of rain washed away his drawing. "It's going to be in a race, though. Somebody better holler *Go!*"

Half the guys piled back into the stake trucks and went with Scotty to the river, to fill sandbags and ferry them back.

Mr. Caldwell and I split the other guys into two crews. The smaller group opened up the diversion channel at the top end and used the first of the sandbags to block the creek from feeding the reservoir.

The bigger group laid into the bank with picks and shovels where Mr. Caldwell said to, digging an eight-foot-wide gap. I worked with them, and it was mean, dangerous, sloppy work, what with the rain and mud sloshing every which way.

Mr. Caldwell shuttled between us and the spillway. Every time he came back, he looked more worried.

Finally, when we'd dug the gap almost down to water level, he said, "All right. That's as far as you can take it until we get the sandbag crew up here."

He and I clambered down the bank and hurried to them. They'd formed a long line and were passing sandbags along it as fast as they could, but the wall they'd got built seemed pitifully small. Not long enough. Only two bags high.

"Can't they do just one more tier?" I asked. "And extend it out some?"

Mr. Caldwell answered, "I'd like them to, but the way the rain's pouring down, I'm afraid to chance it. Even a little bit more pressure might prove too much for that spillway. You want to call them?"

No, I didn't want to. I wanted them to keep laying sandbags.

But they were my guys. They trusted me to take care of them.

Making a megaphone with my hands, I shouted, "Mr. Caldwell says that's it. Let's go!"

He made us all retreat to the road above the reservoir. "I know you want to see," he said, "but I'm not positive what will happen when we break further into that bank. I don't want anybody swept away."

"Who's going to breach it?" Apple asked.

"Mr. Caldwell and me," Scotty said.

"But that's not right," Apple and I said, at exactly the same time.

"Look," I argued, "if there's scrambling to be done, we're...that is, you're..."

"What Moss is trying to say," Sam said, "is that it's a job for guys who can move fast."

Maybe we'd have kept arguing, except, impossible as it seemed, the rain picked up even harder.

"All right," Mr. Caldwell said. "All right. We can't waste time talking. Moss, you know the boys. Pick somebody."

He made Apple and me tie ropes securely around our waists, and he made sure the other ends were held tight by whole gangs of guys.

"Now go easy," he told us. "All you've got to do is get a start. Once the water sees it's free, it's going to make a run through that bank like you're not going to believe."

"I won't say I'm not scared," I told Apple, as we got ourselves into position, down in the gap.

"I know I am," he answered. "You got a good footing?"

"Yeah." I looked behind, to the rest of the guys. "And they've got our safety lines taut. Let's do it."

I swung the pick and he shoveled out mud and flung it away. Down and down we picked and shoveled, till a rivulet of water crossed in front of my foot, different from the way the rain was muddling.

"Up!" I yelled. We leaped for the bank, and once on it I leaned down and scratched my pick along the rivulet. A course of water followed, and then a whole chunk of earth broke free, and then all creation broke loose.

Or that's how it seemed.

The water yanked the pick out of my hands as Apple dragged me backward. And then we were both running from the waterfall we'd started.

Mr. Caldwell wouldn't let any of us—not even himself—go find out what had happened until the reservoir's water level was down to the level of the land where the bank had been broken through. Then, in a sudden letup of rain, Mr. Caldwell said, "Well, who wants to go look?"

All 160 of us slogged out through the wet fields toward the berm.

Please, I thought, as I climbed up on top, *don't let it be as bad as I expect.* Then I looked...

First I saw the spillway, no more broken than it had been.

Then I looked toward the Lundgrens' place, where curving rows of earth glistened with water. Between all the rows of water, there were rows of plants.

I was too far away to see how bad the rain had pounded them, but one thing was sure. The plants, and the topsoil they were growing in, hadn't been washed away.

I was still looking when three people rode out onto the field. They got off their horses and walked among the plants, bending down here and there.

Then one of them got back on his horse and trotted toward us. The way Nate held himself and the way he pranced his horse said it all—the wheat and barley had pulled through.

As had most of the plants around the reservoir. Willow starts still stood upright. A bird was already flitting among them, investigating.

"So," Mr. Caldwell said, pausing for a long pull on his pipe, "it looks like you boys saved the day." He'd come back to camp with us, and we were just finishing up supper.

I didn't know if Captain Hakes had ordered the cooks back to work or if they'd just gone back, but we'd sure eaten good.

I asked, "Do you think the reservoir can be fixed?"

"Sure. We'll have to drain it, rebuild the spillway, repair the break in the bank. It's all doable, though you fellows staying on for second hitches will have your work cut out."

He glanced around. "I hope a lot of you will be."

Chapter 37

The following Friday evening, B Barracks was a scene of confusion worse than I'd ever seen. About thirty fellows would be leaving for good the next morning, and the rest of us would be heading off on the leaves the CCC gave the guys who were reenrolling.

I was reeling with all the things that were happening.

Alerted by Mr. Caldwell, Major Garrett and a couple of other officers had swooped into camp the day after the crisis at the dam. Even Sam didn't hear what all got said over at headquarters, but before they left a lot of changes got made or promised.

One was that Captain Hakes was being relieved of duty, and Major Garrett was going to come back to take his place until a new commander could be assigned.

And something else that happened was that the sheriff came around questioning guys about supplies and inventories. Rumors flew fast, especially after the *Monroe Herald* ran a front-page headline saying 'Local Man Investigated in Camp Scandal.'"

"Do you think Schieling will go to jail?" Apple asked.

"Whatever happens, he's gotten his last government contract," Sam said.

"And I guess he's finished in Monroe," Apple added.

"I don't know about that," Nate said. "Maggie says bad apples have a way of turning up. No offense."

"None taken," Apple said. "Maggie wasn't meaning me."

Because it was the last night of our hitches, everybody had things to say to each other—foolishness mostly. "I better not see you on the fed's Most Wanted list." And, "Romeo, you going to invite me home to meet all those sisters?"

We signed each other's Cold Day Camp yearbooks, which had come back from the printer that day.

You could tell Sam was right proud of them.

Hal had got great photos of all the guys, as well as of scenes around camp and on the work site. There I was, next to Bill Compton, just after the staff pictures.

Sam had tied the whole thing together with a narrative of our six months, and like he'd said he would, he'd included events from the world outside camp.

"It's a fine yearbook," I told him and meant it.

We were interrupted by Sketch, who came over with a folder he gave me. "I thought you might like to have these," he said.

I opened it and saw a drawing of Apple, Nate, Sam, and me in our CCC denims. Sketch had got every single one of our expressions better than any camera could.

"Thanks," I said. "It's great."

"I'm glad you got your armband back," he told me. "It adds a certain something to the picture."

"Just like Apple's," I said.

Because Apple was a junior leader now, too. Major Garrett had offered the job to him the same day he'd returned my armband to me. Apple would be taking over A Barracks when our new hitches started.

Compton had chosen not to reenroll.

"Hey," Apple said, looking over my shoulder, "what's the other picture?"

I pulled it out. This one, instead of being a pencil drawing, was a watercolor picture of the prettiest little lake, stopped up by a low, earthen dam at one end.

Sketch had shown it in springtime, with full-grown willow trees on its banks, leafing out above black-eyed Susans. He'd painted a red-winged blackbird perched on a cattail, and a meadowlark on a fence post off to one side. You could just see a farm field in the distance.

He said, "I guess that one's not so much for remembering as for looking ahead."

The barracks didn't settle down until late, and there was a general understanding that lights-out wasn't going to be enforced. Still, eventually guys finished up their packing, and noisy excitement gave way to quieter talks. I think that was when it really hit everyone that after this, we wouldn't ever all be together again.

Apple, usually the one who could be counted on for a laugh, seemed especially subdued. Finally he said, "We did some pretty good work, huh? Or got a good start, anyway. I mean, it doesn't seem like such a big thing, just building a small reservoir and helping some farmers along, but..."

Sam said, "But you add it to all the other ponds and parks the CCCs are building, and add in the fire lookouts going up on mountaintops and picnic grounds being fixed up and grazing land being restored, and it becomes a big thing."

"It's odd," Apple said, still struggling for words. "I mean, to think that one day we won't be here, but that something we did might be. See, I guess I'm wondering, what if we've already done the most important thing we'll ever do?"

Sam, using newspapers to wrap a breakable, paused to read a story. The headline was something about Hitler's troops in the Rhineland. "Who knows?" he said. "Maybe. Or maybe there's something bigger ahead, and all this is just preparing us for it."

And then all the chatter stopped, as Jimmy and Stan began playing their guitars. Nate got out his harmonica and Hal started softly singing. The last thing I would remember of that night was how, one after another, the guys picked up the song until we were all singing together.

It took all the trucks to get everybody to the train station the next morning. I rode in with Sam to see him off. It should have been a good last chance to visit, but somehow we couldn't get past starts and stops of talk.

And at the station, when his train was about ready to go, all I could think of to say was, "So, Senator, good luck."

"You, too, Trawnley."

It was a pretty sorry exchange for a pair of good friends, but I couldn't for the life of me figure out how to improve on it.

The train whistle sounded and a conductor called, "All aboard. All aboard."

Suddenly Sam gave me a big hug and then, fast as that, he was gone.

I'd planned to see the train off, but I just couldn't. I gave a general wave at the guys packed in it, and then headed for the trucks, walking as fast as I could.

Apple and I had us a great time in Yellowstone, hiking around the bubbling mud pots and watching the geysers shoot off. He flirted some with a waitress in the big lodge there, and I wrote Beatty two postcards.

I aimed to return to Muddy Springs once my second hitch was done, and I wanted her to be there, waiting for me.

Then Apple and I returned to camp early to meet the new fellows. The morning they were to arrive, we headed out to get a couple of stake trucks to bring them back in. Sergeant Ruffino and a corporal had already gone ahead in a car.

Apple got behind the wheel of one truck, and Beggar jumped onto the seat beside him. I climbed into the other truck, started the motor, and saw the gas gauge sitting on empty. "You go on," I called. "I've got to swing by the fuel pump."

Waiting for the tank to fill, I looked out over the silent camp. "Don't worry," I told Thief, who was watching me warily. "Beggar's coming back."

It was a bluebird day—clear skies, warm sun, growing things everywhere. As different as could be from the bleak night I first saw the camp, when it wasn't anything but tents and piles of raw lumber.

Now it was a finished place. A home, really. Mine, anyway, for now.

On my way out, I stopped to straighten the COLD DAY CAMP sign at the entrance. And while there, I took a moment to admire the rock monument. I remembered how carefully we'd put our initials in the concrete.

There was Apple's E. D. I could just hear him saying,

I'm kind of proud of this camp... I want it official. I
had a hand.

Him, and all of us. There wasn't a nickname anyplace.

I got into Monroe just as the train pulled in. By the
time I'd parked, the first new enrollees were already
milling about the station platform, their hands full
with suitcases and duffle bags, guitars and... Was that
really a bag of golf clubs?

I guessed so, judging from the look on Apple's face.

Well, there had to be a story behind that boy, I
thought, as Beggar went to investigate.

And wouldn't Beatty get a tickle, when I wrote her
we'd got a fellow thought he was coming to a country club.

The new guys, fresh from conditioning camp, were
a skinny, weak-looking lot, for sure, but that would
change. Three squares a day and steady work in the
outdoors would do the trick.

I pulled back my shoulders and waded into the
crowd as a kid who reminded me of Romeo came over.
Fifteen? Not even. Face like peach fuzz, except for
what looked like a knife scar down one side.

"You in charge?" he demanded. " 'Cause I've got a
complaint."

"In time," I said, directing him to one of the trucks.
"Let's get you to camp first, and then I'll hear your
story."

He was another who'd have one. I was sure of that. They all would.

He just didn't know how his story was about to change.

"Hey," I called after him.

He turned back.

"Glad to have you here," I said. "We've got us a job to do."

Selected References and Suggestions for Further Reading

CIVILIAN CONSERVATION CORPS

Books

Cohen, Stan. *The Tree Army: A Pictorial History of the Civilian Conservation Corps, 1933–1942.* Missoula, MT: Pictorial Histories Publishing Company, 1980, rev. 1993.

Ermentrout, Robert Allen. *Forgotten Men: The Civilian Conservation Corps.* Smithtown, NY: Exposition Press, 1982.

Holland, Kenneth, and Frank Ernest Hill. *Youth in the CCC.* Washington, DC: American Council on Education, 1942.

Lacy, Leslie Alexander. *The Soil Soldiers: The Civilian Conservation Corps in the Great Depression.* Radnor, PA: Chilton Book Company, 1976.

Merrill, Perry H. *Roosevelt's Forest Army: A History of the Civilian Conservation Corps, 1933–1942.* Montpelier, VT: P. H. Merrill, 1981.

Paige, John C. *The Civilian Conservation Corps and the National Park Service, 1933–1942: An Administrative History.* N.p.: National Park Service, U.S. Department of the Interior, 1985.

Internet Source

National Association of Civilian Conservation Corps Alumni. www.cccalumni.org

THE DEPRESSION:
MONTANA AND RURAL LIFE IN THE 1930S

Books

Agee, James, and Walker Evans. *Let Us Now Praise Famous Men.* Boston: Houghton Mifflin, 1941.

Evans, Walker. *Walker Evans: Photographs for the Farm Security Administration, 1935–1938: A Catalog of Photographic Prints Available from the Farm Security Administration Collection in the Library of Congress.* New York: Da Capo Press, 1973.

Federal Writers' Project of the Work Projects Administration for the State of Montana. *The WPA Guide to 1930s Montana.* Tucson: University of Arizona

Press, 1994. First published as *Montana: A State Guide Book,* 1939 by the Department of Agriculture, Labor and Industry, State of Montana.

Heyman, Therese Thau, Sandra S. Phillips, John Szarkowski, San Francisco Museum of Modern Art. *Dorothea Lange: American Photographs.* San Francisco: Chronicle Books, 1994.

Horan, James D. *The Desperate Years: A Pictorial History of the Thirties.* New York: Bonanza Books, 1962.

Hull, William H. *The Dirty Thirties: Tales of the Nineteen Thirties During Which Occurred a Great Drought, a Lengthy Depression and the Era Commonly Called The Dust Bowl Years.* Edina, MN: William H. Hull, 1989.

Low, Ann Marie. *Dust Bowl Diary.* Lincoln, NE: University of Nebraska Press, 1984.

Merrill, Andrea, and Judy Jacobson. *Montana Almanac.* Helena, MT: Falcon, 1997.

Murphy, Mary. *Hope in Hard Times: New Deal Photographs of Montana, 1936–1942.* Helena, MT: Montana Historical Society Press, 2003.

Reid, Robert L., ed. *Back Home Again: Indiana in the Farm Security Administration Photographs, 1935–1943.* Bloomington, IN: Indiana University Press, 1987.

Rothstein, Arthur. *The Depression Years as Photographed by Arthur Rothstein.* New York: Dover Publications, 1978.

Spritzer, Don. *Roadside History of Montana*. Missoula, MT: Mountain Press, 1999.

Toole, K. Ross. *Twentieth-Century Montana: A State of Extremes*. Norman, OK: University of Oklahoma Press, 1972.

Reader Chat Page

1. Moss Trawnley doesn't plan on getting fired from his job at the airport, but it gives him the freedom to join the CCC, an experience that changes his life. Have you ever had an experience where your life changed or you discovered something new about yourself because things didn't go as you had planned?

2. After Moss and his father spend the night in jail, the justice of the peace asks Moss if he wants to turn out like his dad. Why do you think Moss chooses not to follow in his father's footsteps? What might he have been thinking?

3. Moss lies about his age so that he can get into the CCC. Do you think this is wrong? Why or why not?

4. Moss joins the CCC with no idea of what he'll find, or even where he will be going. What motivates him to make such a drastic decision?

5. In Montana, Moss discovers that he has a talent for deciphering complicated blueprints. What talents do you possess? How did you discover them?

6. When Major Garrett offers Moss the position of junior leader, Moss is flattered, but scared that he is too young for the job. What qualities do you think make a good leader?

7. After Moss goes against Compton's orders and uses the CCC bulldozers to help the townspeople get to their livestock after the big storm, Compton takes all of the credit for the idea. Why do you think Compton does this? What might he find threatening about Moss?

8. What do you think are the most important things that Moss learned during the time he spent at the Cold Day Camp? How do his experiences at the camp change his future?